T0086528

THE
LEGENDARY
LESBIAN
LOTHARIO

THE
LEGENDARY LESBIAN LOTHARIO

the Chronicles of Lilith

BOOK 1

S. C. HELTON

THE LEGENDARY LESBIAN LOTHARIO
BOOK 1

Copyright © 2021 S. C. Helton.

All rights reserved. No part of this book may be used or reproduced by any means, graphic, electronic, or mechanical, including photocopying, recording, taping or by any information storage retrieval system without the written permission of the author except in the case of brief quotations embodied in critical articles and reviews.

This is a work of fiction. All of the characters, names, incidents, organizations, and dialogue in this novel are either the products of the author's imagination or are used fictitiously.

iUniverse books may be ordered through booksellers or by contacting:

iUniverse
1663 Liberty Drive
Bloomington, IN 47403
www.iuniverse.com
844-349-9409

Because of the dynamic nature of the Internet, any web addresses or links contained in this book may have changed since publication and may no longer be valid. The views expressed in this work are solely those of the author and do not necessarily reflect the views of the publisher, and the publisher hereby disclaims any responsibility for them.

Any people depicted in stock imagery provided by Getty Images are models, and such images are being used for illustrative purposes only.
Certain stock imagery © Getty Images.

ISBN: 978-1-6632-2436-1 (sc)
ISBN: 978-1-6632-2435-4 (e)

Library of Congress Control Number: 2021911843

Print information available on the last page.

iUniverse rev. date: 06/10/2021

I am more than half persuaded that I am a man's soul put by some freak of nature into a woman's body ... because I have fallen in love with so many pretty girls and never once the least bit with any man.

—Louisa May Alcott (in an interview
with Louise Chandler Moulton)

CHAPTER 1
LILITH MADE ME DO IT

When Dad was convicted of insider trading, Mom divorced him and moved us to her mother's house in Fort Worth, Texas. We descended into the inferno that is Texas with secrets. Mom devoutly prayed that no one in Fort Worth would find out that her daughter was a notorious deviant back in New York. I just hoped no one found out I was a murderer.

I had no idea how idyllic my life was until the day a worthless piece of shit named Frank Stone raped me on my way home from school. He jumped me from behind (the fucking coward) and hit me on the head with his gun. When I came to, he was thrusting into me and grunting like a pig. He had lain the gun on the ground while I was unconscious. Presumably, he needed both hands to strip my designer jeans off me.

When he had finished what he had come to do, he stood up and wiped my blood off his dick with my underwear. Then the dumb motherfucker remembered the gun … which was in my hand. For the briefest moment, I thought about what Saint Agnes would say. "Leave vengeance to your heavenly father." Then a voice I would later identify as Lilith said, "Where was your heavenly father when that creep besmirched you?"

I shot him twice in the chest. Then I shot his dick off. Then I shot him between the eyes. I kept shooting until the gun was just clicking.

My house was next to the eighth hole of the Meadowbrook Golf Course. The grove of trees where I was attacked was planted fifteen years ago to protect the houses in my neighborhood from shanked golf balls. Beyond the trees was a creek. My dad had built a bridge across the creek just for his little princess. I was halfway across the bridge when my parents came running out to investigate the gunshots.

Mom abruptly stopped and screamed, "Alys!"

I saw the next-door neighbor hurry out to her back yard and cover her little girl's eyes and rush her into the house. The day before, we had both been little girls who played together. Now, I was covered in some man's blood with a gun in my hand.

Daddy knelt by me and gently took the gun from my hand. "Oh, my poor girl. My poor little girl."

The reason I was walking home across the golf course that day was that I had been forced to leave Marymount. I hadn't been expelled or anything so vulgar as that, but it was made quite clear that I was no longer welcome there. At Marymount, I was known as the queer who had attacked Bea Inouye.

Beatrice Inouye was the most beautiful girl in the ninth grade. She looked like a Polynesian goddess. "Beatrice" comes from the Latin "Beatrix," which means "she who makes happy." It was the perfect name for her. Everybody called her Bea. She would flit from here to there spreading happiness. I was madly in love with her. I would have done anything, absolutely *anything* that Beatrice wanted.

In summer 1985, I went to a slumber party at Beatrice's house to celebrate her sixteenth birthday.

"Come here," Beatrice whispered to me. "I want to show you something."

We left the other girls watching the Friday night movie on NBC. Beatrice giggled as she led me past her bedroom and into her older brother's room. "Come see what I've found."

She pulled several *Playboy* magazines out from under her brother's bed. "Look."

I didn't know what airbrushing was then, and I was amazed that the people at *Playboy* could find so many perfect, flawless women. I felt sorry for them though. Every one of them had enormous breasts. I've had the same burden since I was thirteen, and I knew what a pain they could be.

Bea pointed at one of the nudes. "Hers are no bigger than yours."

I smiled my thanks and kept flipping through the pages.

"Are they?" she persisted.

I looked at her closely, and there was no question in my mind what Bea wanted me to do. I quickly unbuttoned my blouse and reached behind me and unhooked my bra. I let the bra fall to the floor. Bea stared at my breasts hungrily. For the first time in her life, she was unsure. "Can I …"

"Do anything you want," I told my love. I leaned into her. My mouth was nearly touching her ear. "I'll do anything you want me to," I whispered.

She reached out, tentatively at first, and softly stroked my firm breasts. We were both beginning to breath hard. Her tongue tipped my erect nipple. I found she was wearing no bra under her pajamas. She didn't need support. Her breasts were perfect—small and firm.

I reached between her legs. She was already wet. "Do you want me to …"

"Yes, Alys. *Yes!*"

I kissed my way down her rib cage. I kissed her tiny tummy and licked her belly button. I pulled her panties down over her slim hips. When I placed my lips on her pudendum, I felt a joy I'd never known. *This is what I'm here for*, I marveled. *This is what I was born for.*

She moaned when my tongue darted out and licked her virgin skin. Her moaning grew louder as my cunning tongue parted her opening.

Suddenly, a bloodcurdling scream almost made me pee myself. Could I have hurt her?

No. It was her mother who had screamed, and right behind her were all the girls from the party.

Mrs. Inouye was the senior senator from Hawaii. She had been a power in D.C. since the days of the Kennedys. She was a devout Catholic. Needless to say, she took a dim view of her daughter getting cunnilingus from the dirty blond daughter of a shady businessman and his social- climbing Southern wife. I just hope her ire didn't have any connection with the harsh sentence he was given.

So, I had to transfer to Trinity. Trinity was no Marymount. But on the plus side, it was within walking distance to our house—just across the golf course and up the hill. Of course, it didn't take long before the kids at Trinity were whispering about the dyke who had been caught giving a muff job to a girl as a birthday present.

I didn't care. No, really, I had a plan. I was going to write a novel about Henry VIII's fourth wife, Cat Howard. (I think she was the fourth—anyway, the young slutty one.) With the royalties from my best-selling novel, I would live on the West Coast and date starlets.

The judge wanted to let me go scot-free. "I wish you had just shot him in the knee," he said. "We wouldn't even be here today. But since you got your trigger finger stuck, I'm going to have to give you six months in juvenile for unauthorized use of a firearm." That's how I got sent to the Spiro T. Agnew Juvenile Facility in Newark, New Jersey.

While I was in "Spiro T," I heard that Beatrice had been forgiven by the stern (male) god of the Catholics for allowing herself to be seduced by evil (yours truly). She was the innocent victim and had become even more popular. That was all right; if they wanted to brand me with a scarlet Q, let 'em. I just wanted Bea to look me in the face and tell me it had meant nothing to her.

Mom got me out a couple of months early by promising the state of New York she was moving me to Texas. I used the opportunity to get drunk and crash the Marymount homecoming party.

Bea's date was the star quarterback (and alpha male) Jack Hardy. He was quite certain that Beatrice would have sex with him after the party because he had thrown three touchdowns. In male-parlance, three touchdowns equal sexual intercourse. (One touchdown was a guarantee of no more than a blow job.)

I was quite certain that Bea would have sex with him because she was desperate to prove that she was a normal heterosexual. I couldn't believe that Bea was consciously aware of this. I wanted to warn her that men just use women for their own pleasure and care nothing about the feelings of the object they are using.

I drank a lot of beers out in Mom's car trying to come up with a clever ruse to get me into the dance. The "clever ruse" proved unnecessary. I solved the problem organically by throwing up on the ticket taker. When she went screaming into the restroom to clean herself up, I sauntered into the dance.

I found Jack and Beatrice, in between dances, standing by the punch bowl.

I staggered up to them and spoke. "This fellow expects you to fuck him tonight."

"Piss off, queer." (This was Jack, not Beatrice.)

"God, Alys. You're covered in vomit." (Beatrice)

"I just want to tell you one thing …"

That was as far as I got. For one thing, I forgot what I was talking about. For another, Jack Hardy grabbed me by the arm and tried to remove me. I kicked him in the nuts. And as his head snapped forward, I punched him in the nose. He landed hard on his back.

I sprang up, brushed my hands nonchalantly, smiled at Beatrice, and threw up in the punch bowl.

Not my finest hour. That would have been an appropriate ending to the story of my first love. But unfortunately, there's an epilogue.

⌇

The kids of Marymount used to gather at Sycamore Park on Friday nights for what they called "watching the submarine races." The guys would borrow the family car, pick up their girlfriends, and park in the dark among the trees around the pond and make out.

On my last night in New York, I sat alone in Mom's car in the brightly lit parking lot watching the shadows and flashes of light as cigarettes were lit. I had followed Jack and Bea. I don't know why. After about half an hour, the interior light of Jack's car came on and Bea exited. She was so drunk she could barely get her underpants on. The bra was, apparently, too much trouble. She discarded it in the weeds. She staggered toward the outdoor restrooms the park provided.

Jack got out of the car after her. Holding a beer in one hand and his cock in the other, he pissed on the side of the car. As he did so, he peered into the back window.

"Atta girl, Brenda, suck him good!" he crowed.

Bea managed to make it halfway to the building that housed the toilets and then fell. I ran to her. She was on her hands and knees but seemed unable to rise any further. I helped her up.

"Hey, little Buzz Bee, are you alright?"

She squinted and recognized me. Her eyes cleared, and she smiled at me. Then they clouded over, and she sobbed, "Oh, Leesy, what have I done?"

CHAPTER 2

FAUSTIAN HUBRIS

When Lilith first spoke to me, she sounded a bit like Janis Joplin trying to sing "Me and Bobby McGee" with half a bottle of whiskey sloshing around in her hand. The second time I heard her she sounded more like Julie Andrews singing, "Spoonful of Sugar." I was tossing and turning in my bed and trying not to think about things like suicide and such.

"Sorry about that."

I knew who was speaking.

"Sorry? You're sorry? You tell me that piece of shit slime bucket deserves to die, and then when I've killed a human being and am branded with the "mark of Cain," you say sorry?"

"You know, I didn't actually say any of that. The thing is, I've been spouting my opinions for ten thousand years, and you are the first person who's heard me."

I tried rolling over on my side, facing the wall. I've never counted sheep, but I've got this thing where the Rockettes put on a private show just for me ... without panties.

"It's the biggest thing to happen to me in the last thousand years," Lilith continued. "That was when I came into this life as a non-corporeal entity. Life is so much better when you don't have to eat or go to the bathroom or anything like that."

"Are you still here?"

"Sorry, it's just that I've always dreamed of the day when I could communicate with womankind. With your help, I think I can save humanity; that's all. I just thought you might be interested."

"What's in it for me?"

"Wow. I'm shocked, Alys. I knew you were one of the most self-involved people I've seen in the last five hundred years, but the shallowness of your character is truly shocking. Surely, you can see that the end of humanity affects you personally?"

"You say the world is coming to an end. People have been saying that since Hector was a pup. Still ain't happened. Who the hell are you, anyway?"

"I am *Lilith, first woman, born of the clay, daughter of god, equal of Adam, mother of humanity.*"

"Glad to meet you. I'm Alys, daughter of Fran and Scott Loxley."

Minutes passed. Twenty-five Rockettes kicked their feet up in the air. Twenty-six.

"So, if you could have anything, what would you wish for?"

I rolled around quickly, hoping to catch a glimpse of her. I had hoped she would ask this. "I want Beatrice Inouye to kneel before me on the Betsy Ross Auditorium stage with the entire student body of Marymount High School in the audience. I want her to beg me to allow her to kiss my feet.

I want to say, 'No, you may not' and turn around and raise up my dress—"

"Whoa! That's a disturbing and obsessively specific wish. How about this? How about if I make you irresistible to women?"

"You're shitting me."

"I shit you not."

"Hey! Wait a minute. Do you think I was born yesterday? I read Dr. Faustus when I was thirteen. You want my soul, don't you?"

"Alys, if you were half as smart as you think you are, you would know that you couldn't give away your soul even if you wanted to."

"Yeah? Well, if you were smart, you wouldn't end a sentence with a preposition."

"Fine. Good luck ever getting laid."

"Wait. What about the really pretty ones? What about the popular girls?"

"*All* of them, Alys! All the little fishies in the sea—short ones, tall ones, blind ones, kind ones."[1]

I was bouncing on the bed on my knees. "Do I have to sign in blood, or what?"

"All you gotta do, kid, is tell the people my story."

"And what *is* your story? What is the story of Lilith?"

"It's a tragic love story to start. It's also the biggest crime caper any 'Mickey Spillane' could have imagined. Most of all, kid, it's the exposition of the biggest criminal conspiracy in the history of the world—a conspiracy that subjugated half the population of the world for over two thousand years."

"Hey, if you can make me irresistible to women, I'll gladly write a biography for you. Can you just wait until I've finished the one about Cat Howard?"

"I don't want you to write a book, Alys. I want you to start a new church. I want you to be the rock upon which the Church of Lilith is founded."

～✐～

---

[1] Mitch Ryder and the Detroit Wheels

My grandmother has never forgiven my mother for marrying Scott Loxley. Apparently, he was in the luggage business when he eloped with Mom because Grandmother constantly complains about "Francesca running off with that carpetbagger." She won't forgive Mom, and she won't provide any money for my education. That means public school for me. Mom has enrolled me in Handley High School. (Go, Horny Toads.)

My first day at school, I discover that Mom has signed me up for tennis. I sigh. It's sad when parents use a child to fight old battles. I see this clearly as Mom's last coup de grâce in her war with Dad. I see her placing the blade of her sword in the chinks of Dad's armor and saying, "Guess what? She's playing tennis, not studying taekwondo" as she shoves the blade into his heart. I used to think that they were fighting over me, but I sometimes suspect that it goes back farther than that.

I went looking for Mom to tell her I wasn't playing on the tennis team. I was disappointed but not surprised to find her flirting with the principal, Peter Peterskin. This was the guy Dad had stolen her away from sixteen years ago. Mom was obviously just going to erase the last sixteen years and start over. There was no way I was ever going to "erase" my feelings for Dad.

When that "incident" happened, I asked Dad again to let me take taekwondo. I had begun to ask him to let me take martial arts instead of tennis when I had an unfortunate "growth spurt" when I was thirteen. I had gone from a training bra to a 36DD in one year. After the ... you know, he put his foot down. Like the vastly outnumbered English archers at Agincourt, Dad stood up to Mom and declared that I would choose whatever sport I wanted to take. The "compromise" was that I ended up taking both. It was another expense for Dad to cover. It wasn't a whole lot, but I must ask myself, Could the extra classes have been the straw that broke the camel's back?

At some point, Dad must have realized that he wasn't going to be able to take care of his family in the style to which they were accustomed without cutting some corners. I know Dad loves me. I know he would have done anything for his little princess. Did he break the law to get me into Marymount? Did he feel embarrassment at my departure? Did he think of me as a disgrace to the Loxley name? And did I unintentionally make his punishment worse by falling in love with a powerful woman's daughter? These are the things that were on my mind as I walked through the halls of Handley High my first day.

I turned a corner and saw a beautiful Hispanic girl being accosted.

This Hispanic Helen of Troy was surrounded by three extremely irate girls. The one in the hot pants and mesh stockings was right in her face. "You stay away from him! He's mine. Don't make me cut you, bitch!"

I had promised Mom I wouldn't fight any more. But at that point, Hot Pants pulled out a knife. She grabbed a handful of the beautiful girl's hair and threatened to hack it off.

Sorry, Mom, but this is unacceptable!

I ran in and chopped the knife out of her hand. Using my own weight as leverage, I threw her over my head. She hit the lockers with a satisfying crash.

The dark-haired beauty nonchalantly buffed her nails. "Thanks, Galahad. I owe you one."

"Tell me your name. and we'll call it even."

"My name is Martha Mendoza. This is not the first time I've been rescued, but it IS the first time I've been rescued by a little slip of a girl, like you. That girl over there trying to pick herself up off the floor is at least four inches taller than you and outweighs you by thirty pounds. How did you do that?"

"It's basically just a matter of leverage."

"Oh? Modest, too? What's your name, modest superhero?"

"My name is Alys. So, why did that girl attack you?"

"She thought I was trying to steal her boyfriend. Hell, I didn't know he was her boyfriend. If girls don't want me talking to their boyfriend, they should put a collar on 'em, you know? Like 'this is Linda's man' or 'property of Mary,' right? What about you, Alys? You got a boy I need to stay away from?"

I didn't want to lie to Martha. "No, don't worry. I hate boys."

"You hate boys? Does that mean you love girls?"

I nodded.

"Wait. Seriously, you like to fuck girls?"

I looked her right in the eye. "I haven't done it yet, but I think so."

A moment passed.

"Martha, do you think we could be friends?"

"Be friends with a puta? Are you kidding me?"

I was determined not to cry in front of this beautiful girl. "OK. I understand."

"You big dummy! I'm just joking with you. Come here and give me a hug. Of course, we're friends. I like you. You're honest. You're fun. You can hurl big girls over tall buildings. Look, there's my boyfriend."

Martha ran up to a big, muscular guy. He was about six three. He wore a greasy ball cap that said "John Deere" on it. He had on a dirty T-Shirt, blue jeans, and scuffed work boots. He extended a huge hand with dirt under the fingernails.

"I'm Allen Freemont. Glad to meet you."

"I'm Alys. Nice to meet you, Allen."

"She's my new best friend," Martha said. "She's gay. We have to help her find a girlfriend."

"OK," Allen said, with (I swear) a guffaw. "But I don't think there are any other lesbians at Handley High."

From the mouths of babes.

I don't like the word "gay." The word used to mean lighthearted and carefree. "Gay" was Gene Kelly dancing and "Singing in the Rain." Now, it denotes sexual preference. I think gaiety died in WWI, along with twenty million human beings—RIP.

Nevertheless, I am pigeon-holed into that category. I'm gay, even if I'm morose. And that is strike one against me in the ubiquitous high school popularity rating.

Oh, don't kid yourself. If you are in high school, you are on the list. If you say you're not, or that you don't care about that stuff, that just puts you further down the list.

Strike two for me is that I'm what Martha would call a "chica mas loco." I believe if those goddamn windmills won't stand down, we must tilt them. I believe justice is possible in this world, and I'm going to form a gang of vigilantes to make it happen.

Strike three against me is that I'm not patriotic. I'm not particularly unpatriotic. I just don't think we are the greatest nation that ever existed or ever will exist. I'm a secular humanist. I believe in humanity. I believe we have a fighting chance to survive for another millennium if we can drop all the bullshit and tell each other the truth.

Nevertheless, being number one on the popularity rating list is nothing to having a friend. And now I had a friend.

CHAPTER 3

VIRGIL GUIDES ME THROUGH THE UNDERWORLD

One of the dumb things my grandmother says is, "It never rains, but it pours." My first two weeks at Handley, I thought I'd never make a friend. Now I have two. The second one is (unbelievably) a boy.

Fort Worth is famous for its Stock Show. Every year, farmers from all over the state bring their horses, cows, sheep, and the like to be judged. I don't know who the judges are, but I know they're required to wear white ten-gallon hats and pointy cowboy boots. The livestock is paraded around and ogled by the judges, blue ribbons and oversized checks are passed around, and the winners are taken off to be slaughtered and eaten or put out to stud.

When sophomore girls enter the hallowed halls of Handley High, the sons of breeders conduct a similar contest. The upperclassmen hang around the entrance to the school and discuss the new class of prime meat.

"Look at the udders on that one, Jed!"

"How'd you like to ride *that* heifer?"

Seniors make bets on which ones they will deflower and how long it will take them.

How do you think the proud daughters of Texans react? Would you believe they get all red and embarrassed as if they had done something inappropriate? Unbelievable!

And I'm not even going to mention those who simpered and acted pleased to be objectified like a piece of meat. Forget those whores! I'm talking about the nice girls. I mean, what's wrong with this picture? Are Southern girls taught to be meek and submissive to men, even when those men are dicks?

One dumbass yokel felt he was entitled to check out the merchandise tactilely. He squeezed one of my breasts. I punched him in the stomach and kneed him in the nose. His cronies surrounded me. Suddenly, this nice-looking guy with a Kurt Vonnegut paperback in his back pocket was by my side, fists clenched.

The cowardly cowboys drug the touchy boy away.

"Thanks," I said.

He smiled and walked off.

He seemed shy and gentle, almost nice enough to be a girl.

My therapist had told me I needed to get over my antipathy toward men.

I caught up to the guy and said, "And so it goes." His face went blank for a second, and then he smiled and said, "Oh, yeah, this." He pulled *Cat's Cradle* out of his pocket.

"I also liked *The Sirens of Titan*," I told him. "Say, I'm new here. Could you tell me how to get to Miss Wimple's biology class?"

By the time we got to my biology class, we had surprised ourselves with the discovery that we had both read and enjoyed *God Bless You, Mr. Rosewater.*

"Well, this is me," I said. "I think today we're going to learn why the dinosaurs went extinct. What's your next class?"

"I have Miss Moore's world history."

"Um. We passed that about six classrooms ago."

"Oh, fuck. I MEAN 'DANG'! Sorry. I'm sorry, I ..."

The poor guy did a complete 360 and then another 180 and stumbled down the hall.

I turned to go into my class, and I heard, "*Hey.*"

I turned back around.

He yelled, "What's your name?"

"My name is Alys."

"*What?*" He hurried back to me. He dropped one of his textbooks, but he just left it. When he was close, he repeated, "What's your name?"

"I'm Alys Loxley."

"How do you spell that?" he asked. Then he blushed. He turned around and bumped into a senior girl.

"Watch where you're going, nerd."

"Yeah. Sure, sorry. OK." He took one step and then turned back to me. Even though we were no more than five feet away from each other, he yelled, "*I'm Virgil.* Virgil Wilder."

When I walked out of class an hour later, Virgil was standing there.

"Sorry." He said, "I just had to know about the dinosaurs. How did they become extinct?"

"They wouldn't fit on the ark."

"Of course."

After a slightly awkward moment, Virgil asked, "Could I walk with you to your next class?"

"I have study-hall down by the gym. Is that on your way?

"Yes. Absolutely."

As we walked, Virgil looked over his glasses at me. "Do you know Sarah Marsh?"

"No. I don't know anyone, really. I'm new."

"Well, Sarah is a little brunette girl who knows everything about everybody. I spent all last period sitting next to her in her French class asking her about you. She tells me that you went to a prep school in New York."

"I thought you had world history last period?"

"I thought I'd sit in on French class today. I hoped to learn something I didn't already know."

"Unlike in Miss Moore's world history class. I get it. Yeah, I went to a prep school last year. So what?"

"The thing is, Alys, there really *are* scholars and intellectuals in Texas. We're all doing what we can, but … well, right now, the school board insists on listing creationism as a theory of human origin. A lot of our teachers won't even teach evolution. I just … well, I just hope you don't think we are all a bunch of rustic hicks."

"Not at all. Your curriculum offers creationism and evolution side by side as theories of human origin. As an agnostic, I totally agree with that approach."

Virgil was peering over his glasses at me, wide-eyed. He bumped into a kid bent over a water fountain. When he recovered his balance, he said, "You're kidding!"

"No. But I don't think that schools should offer only two possible explanations. Why not offer equal opportunity to all theories? Now, my personal favorite is the theory that human beings are the descendants of aliens who colonized the planet millions of years ago. Some sort of cataclysm destroyed their civilization, and the survivors were the cavemen."

"Wait. For real?"

"Well, it would explain the legend of Atlantis and the artwork that only takes shape when seen from the sky. Here's study hall."

"How do UFOs fit into that theory?"

"I'll see you later, Virgil."

"They could be, like, rescue ships who got caught in a time warp and ..." He was still talking about alien theories as I entered the classroom.

I was changing into some cutoffs and a halter top. I thought I'd lounge out by grandmother's pool. I figured I'd earned it after a long day of reading, writing, and interpreting Texas drawl.

"So, how is my church coming along?"

"Goddamn it!" I shrieked. "Don't sneak up on a person like that. Where are you, anyway? Are you in my head? You weren't here last night when I was fantasizing about Phoebe Cates, were you?"

"Don't worry, kid. I have better things to do than hang around a teenage girl. And I'll always announce myself when I *do* arrive. So, how close are we to getting my word out?"

"Actually, I did some research on you at the library. You don't have really good press in this world, you know? There's not much about you, and what there is, is uniformly bad. You are generally considered a 'demon of lust' who was cast out of the Garden of Eden. By the way, just between you and me, you didn't have sex with a snake, did you?"

The tree outside my window burst into flame and was instantly consumed down to ash. Lilith was pissed!

"Hey," I said, looking out the window, nervously, "fix that before my grandmother sees it."

The next time I looked, the tree was back to normal, and Lilith was chill.

"It's that blasted Eve. She's been spreading lies about me for ten thousand years now. You know, if you throw enough mud at the wall, some of it is going to stick. Well now, thanks to you, I can finally reveal my side of the story. Do you know why Eve hates me so badly? Do you know why she has slandered and besmirched my good name all these years? It's because she is *jealous*! She is jealous of the fact that I am Adam's legitimate wife—*and his equal*!

"Adam and I were created with the same 'life force' that causes flowers, plants, trees, and grains to grow from the earth. We both had an organ that would 'quicken' and generate life each year. We lived for thousands of years like that. Each of us would have another little human each year. Lesser animals were kept out of the garden and reproduced by the more vulgar method of sexual impregnation.

Then, one terrible day, Adam tripped over a snake that had trespassed into the garden. The fall broke a rib, and the sharp end of the broken rib punctured his reproductive organ. It shriveled up and withered. (Today that organ is called an appendix.) Adam's reproductive juices were rerouted to the dangly thing where he urinated. We were forced to reproduce the way the animals did. Every time his wee-wee (as we called it in those days) became engorged, he would mount me and plant his seed into me. This seemed unfair to me. I felt I was doing the work of two. And quite naturally, I complained.

"Well, in the meantime, that little bitch, Eve, was spying on us and watching us have sex. She became jealous and tried to seduce Adam.

"Can you imagine? I mean, technically, she was his daughter! Of course, we didn't have any laws (or even taboos) against incest at that time, but, come on! That's just wrong! You know what I mean? So, I added this to my list of complaints. Well, you know what happened then."

Wait. What? "No, I don't. Nobody does. You're barely mentioned in the history books. You were kicked out of the garden under a cloak of mystery and roam the world inflaming men with lust."

"Women too. Don't forget women."

"How am I supposed to build a church on such a character?"

"Stop dicking around, Loxley. Do you want to have sex with more women than Wilt Chamberlain or not? Tell me who you want, and I'll give her to you."

"Cathy Anderson," I replied without thinking. "I want Cathy Anderson."

CHAPTER 4

THE IMPERTINENTLY CURIOUS MAN

My job on the tennis team was to volley the ball back and forth with the coaches' darling, Cathy Anderson. I was to place gentle lobs to her forehand and give her an occasional easy backhand shot. I had done my job if she finished a game without breaking a sweat. It was a simple job, and I loved it. Cathy Anderson was the most beautiful girl I'd ever seen. She was tall, blond, and blue-eyed. She reminded me of the girls in Beatrice's brother's *Playboy*.

Martha said I was crazy to even think about her. "She's straight, pendejo. And she's rich."

"So, you're saying it will be tough?"

"I'm saying it's impossible, ya moron! It'll never happen."

Still, she didn't know about my ace in the hole. After my talk with Lilith, I felt confident as I approached Cathy after our first game. She was bent over, hands on knees, breathing heavily, as if she had done something arduous. I sat in a lawn chair next to her. I crossed my strong, athletic legs and showed her a lot of thigh. "Good workout?" I asked.

"Be a dear and fetch me a bottle of water, would you?"

I guess Lilith's old black magic takes some time to work. I fetched her water. When I handed it to her, she said, "Thank you ... um ..."

"Alys."

"Yes, of course." She spotted some of her 1 percent friends and walked off.

Lilith, I thought to myself, *you've got a lot of splaining to do.*

"What did I tell you?" Martha said when I told her about it. "You're not in her league. Don't worry about it, I think I can fix you up with Sarah Marsh. I think she's ambivalent about sex. You might cop a feel."

"Do you know Stanley?" Martha's boyfriend asked.

Martha looked at him as if he had suddenly grown another head. "My boyfriends seldom speak. But when they do, their words are pearls of wisdom. Stanley is an intellectual like you. He might be a way in for you.

On my way to afternoon practice, I "bumped into" Stanley Scovall. He was sitting in the bleachers watching Cathy practice.

Well, he wasn't actually paying any attention to her. He was doing homework (his or hers, I couldn't tell).

"Stanley! Well, hi, it's me, Alys." I was hoping he would remember me from debate club.

But he said, "You're the girl who walks around the hall mumbling to herself and making the odd 'throat-slashing' gesture."

See, the thing is, I'm working on this novel about Cat Howard and the blood-thirsty King Henry VIII, who executed her. It's estimated that Henry executed 57,000 of his subjects in his thirty-six-year reign. One of those was Cat. I get so angry as I go over the dialogue in my mind that I sometimes unconsciously make an 'off-with-her-head' gesture, imagining the cruel king condemning the poor seventeen-year-old girl. So far, it's the only thing that kids at Handley know me for. I'm an oddball.

"Yeah, that's me." Cathy was practicing her serve. I'd never seen her serve before. "Is that her hardest serve, or is she just resting her arm?" I asked.

"Huh? Um. I don't know. Is there something wrong with the way she's serving?"

"No. I just hope that's not all she's got. If it is, she ain't bringing home any trophies for the Horny Frogs."

"Phrynosoma hernandesi, actually. They are nearing extinction due to the extermination of their main food source—red ants."

"They eat red ants, eh? No wonder they're going extinct. They should try crickets or something."

We sat there a while, contemplating the dietary habits of ugly toads.

After a few minutes, Stanley spoke, "Are you friends with Martha Mendoza?"

"Yes I am. She's my bestest friend in all the world."

"Oh. Bestest, huh?" Stanley went back to his homework.

"Why do you ask?"

"Huh? Oh well, you seem like a lovely girl, and I would hate for you to get in with the wrong crowd."

"*What?*"

"Since you are new, you probably wouldn't know, but there are some concerns about her morals."

"Her morals? What bullshit! Hey, is this about the rumor that she blew the entire Handley High basketball team? That is totally false. She didn't blow the whole team. See, what happened—"

"No, that's not it. There is talk of her embezzling lunch money from schoolkids."

"What? No, no, no. That's totally wrong. It's not us ..."

Damn it. This Stanley Scovall is smarter than I had given him credit for. He'd ambushed me and got me to admit I was involved.

It's nothing, folks. It's a very minor league scam on punks who actually *do* steal little kids' lunch money. We strong-arm the strong-armers!

See, a plate lunch costs $3.50 in the cafeteria at the junior high school. Most moms give the kid a five-dollar bill. Bullies take the fiver, right? What we do is, we approach the perp and suggest he return it to us. Usually, a few bats of the eye from the beautiful Martha Mendoza will do the trick. Sometimes I have to provide muscle. At first, I didn't appear to be much of a threat. I'm five foot four and weigh a hundred pounds on a good day. But, gradually, my reputation grew. I'm quite adept at taekwondo, and I hate bullies. I did nothing to quash the rumor that my hands were registered deadly weapons.

The kid gets his lunch money back, Martha keeps the change, I get to see justice done, and the perp learns a valuable lesson in civics. Everyone wins.

Then the "law and order" Nazis get involved. "You are in violation of Article 3 Section 4 of blah, blah, blah." They tell us, "*You* are committing a crime."

"*What about the fucking bullies?*" I didn't realize I had spoken out loud.

Stanley gave the standard answer. "You should let the authorities handle it."

"The authorities don't do shit!" I screamed at Stanley. "The kids won't tell the teachers because they'll get beat up if they do. The bullies know they will have to answer to me if they go after the kid."

"You can't just take the law into your own hands."

That was one cliché too many for me. My pent-up anger exploded. Aware that I was probably blowing any chance I might have with Cathy, I yelled at Stanley, "*We* don't steal We take back! We fight bullies. Goddamn it, Stanley, *we do something*! We don't just shake our heads and say, 'Tsk-tsk, what a shame,' like you rich pussies!"

<hr>

I was sitting in the cafeteria with the little brunette girl. She had made the mistake of asking me a question about our History homework, and I was regaling her with useless information about Tudor England.

"You better believe the Seymours were pimping their daughters just as much as the Boleyns were. It reminds me of a joke: The king asks a lady, 'If I took you for my wife and gave you all the wealth of my kingdom, would you give me great pleasure in our bed?'

"'Of course, Your Majesty. I would please you beyond your wildest dreams. I would do anything you want.'

"'If I give you twenty dollars, will you fuck me?'

"'Sire! What kind of woman do you think I am?'

"'That has already been established,' the king replied."

Martha and her boyfriend sat down at the table with us, and Martha supplied the punchline: "We're just haggling over the price, now."

The little brunette made herself scarce.

"Guess who wants to meet with you?" Martha asked.

"Well, I know it's not Stanley Scovall. I recently called him a pussy."

"Good call," Martha's boyfriend opined.

"No." Martha laughed. It's the Queen of the Handley High School elite, herself, Cathy Anderson. And get this. She asked me not to tell Stanley about it."

"Did she say why she wants to meet me?" I asked.

"Officially, she wants to challenge you to a set of tennis, but we talked for quite a while. And, well, I think she likes you."

My heart jumped up in my throat. (I know that is a cliché, but clichés are popular because they express universal feelings.) "Did she say she likes me?"

Not exactly. She thinks you're funny. She thinks it's cute the way you walk through the halls, deep in thought, doing that cutthroat gesture and saying, 'Off with her head.'"

I was not entirely pleased. Apparently, the queen found me amusing. On the other hand, to be near that beautiful blue-eyed goddess, I would gladly become a court jester. "Why does she want to play tennis?"

"Stanley told her you were criticizing her game. He said you told him you could beat her."

"I never said that."

"So, could you beat her?"

"I could beat her without a racket. That's not the point. I want her to like me. How would she like me if I just beat her at her own sport? I'd prefer a candlelit dinner."

"Well, if you can arrange a candlelit dinner with the most popular (and purportedly straight) girl at Handley High School, go ahead. If you are willing to meet her on the tennis court, you can do it Saturday. She normally practices her singles game on Saturday morning with a girl named Starr. Stanley attends a Young

Republicans meeting every Saturday. Cathy has challenged you to a match."

Bob, Martha's boyfriend, cleared his throat.

"What?" I asked him.

Bob took of his cap and twisted it around in his hands. He looked at Martha and then kicked some dirt.

"Oh hell, Bob," Martha snapped. "I was going to tell her. See, Alys, Cathy is surrounded by sycophants telling her how great she is. She thinks you are just a flunky. She thinks it's a sure thing that she's going to beat you. She's kind of made a big deal out of it. She's calling it 'the War of Northern Aggression.' She'll be wearing a Confederate cap, and you'll be wearing a Yankee cap. The loser goes from the tennis courts to the girl's dressing rooms wearing nothing but their cap."

"It's about half the distance of a football field," Bob said, "in case you were wondering."

〜✐〜

After school, I found Stanley Scovall leaning on the hood of my 1974 Honda Civic. (If you have a lawn mower, you might recognize the motor.)

"You looking for me?" I asked, warily.

"You're a lesbian, right?"

OK. No beating around the bush for Mr. Stanley Scovall. "Yeah, so what?"

"I want you to do me a favor. I would offer you money, but I don't want to insult you. After your passionate diatribe yesterday, I know you are a person of principles. Frankly, if you were the kind of person who would accept money for this favor, you would be the kind of person who would later demand more money for your silence. I trust your discretion."

This was beginning to sound interesting. "What exactly do you want me to do, Stanley?"

"I want you to seduce Cathy."

I called Mom and told her I would not be home for dinner. Stanley drove to the new McDonald's up on Lancaster in his brand-new Volkswagen Beetle.

"I am going to tell you something in complete confidentiality. You would gain nothing by revealing it, but you would wound Cathy deeply."

"I would never do anything to hurt Cathy. I mean it, Stanley. I think she's wonderful."

"OK. It's been Cathy's lifelong dream to be of the nobility. I have made it my lifelong ambition to provide that for her. I have a plan. The essential part of the plan I wouldn't have been able to provide for her, but luckily, providence has already given it to her. I speak of her great beauty. The rest I can do.

"The first thing I will do is arrange a successful political career here in Texas. I will guide her through the political process until she becomes the governor of this great state at the age of thirty. Then her glamour and wealth will attract the nobility of Europe. Believe me, there are many counts and dukes who can't pay their electric bills. They will be flocking to Texas with titles and marriage proposals. She will have her dream come true; I promise you."

"Sounds like a plan."

"Yes. The problem is that, right now, she's a teenage girl. You know how teenage girls are."

"I've heard stories."

"Lately she's become a little ... um, what's the word? 'Bi-curious?' That kind of thing is all well and good—as long as it's handled discreetly. I understand that it happens to college girls all the time. Women have their adventures, their little flings, and then it's back to looking for a husband. No big deal. But Cathy is so popular that she's highly visible. Anything she does is noticed and noted. I can't have that kind of a black mark against her."

"I understand perfectly, Stanley. And I'm 100 percent on board. How do we get started?"

(To those of you who were waiting to see if I would rip his eyes out or just give him a good, old-fashioned lecture on true love, you don't understand my obsession with this girl. I'd make a deal with the devil himself to be with Cathy. I couldn't afford pride.)

"I was thinking we could start a tradition of you coming over to my house on Saturday mornings to play chess. I live right next door to Cathy. I could get called away, leaving the two of you there—"

"Saturdays are not good for me. How about Sundays?"

"Well, I usually watch football on Sundays in the fall."

"Hey, I'm female. I multitask. I can watch the Cowboys and beat you at chess at the same time."

"And Cathy?"

"Just put that on my halftime 'honey-do' list. No problem."

CHAPTER 5

THE BLOODY T-SHIRT

I got up unusually early on the Saturday of the tennis match. I went down the hallway to where it ends in the kitchen. I made myself a good, nutritional breakfast of Pop-Tarts and Dr. Pepper.

You coulda knocked me over with a dildo when I looked down the hall and saw Mr. Peterskin coming out of Mom's bedroom, naked as a jaybird, his dick swinging free in the wind.

When he saw me, a little piss shot out of his semi-engorged penis, and he ducked into the bathroom. I was furious. I slammed into Mom's door so hard it bounced off the wall and swung back and hit me in the arm. (Hurt like a bitch.)

Mom was sitting up in bed, a sheet pulled up over her breasts.

"Hey, you fucking whore," I yelled, "your john just peed on the carpet in the hallway!"

Mom's eyes blazed. All modesty was forgotten. She threw off the sheet and grabbed a robe. As she put it on, she screamed, "You get thrown out of Marymount for publicly diddling a senator's daughter, and you call *me* a whore?"

Self-preservation overcame anger, and I decided to retreat to the kitchen. "Yeah?" I hollered. "Well, did you ever hear the saying, 'Don't fowl your own nest'?"

Mom walked into the kitchen with all the dignity she could muster and began to look in the refrigerator as if she were just making breakfast on a normal day.

"It *is* my nest, and I'll have whatever guests I want. And if you don't like it, you can get your own place."

Do you hate that as much as I do? Parents love to lord it over teens how helpless we are. Their favorite words are "because I say so." Its derivatives, like "because I'm your mother," really chap my ass. They are saying, "We have complete control over you, and you have no rights at all. Even though they constantly chide us for how self-pitying it sounds, it's impossible not to reply, "I didn't ask to be born!"

I think there is a reasonable logic there. The adults choose (usually) to have the children. The children have no say. Therefore, the parents are responsible for ensuring the child's happiness. It makes perfect sense to me. All I gotta do now is go out and find some teenage lawyer to write up the law.

Mom took a dozen eggs out of the refrigerator and set them on the counter. Evidently, she was making eggs for breakfast. She was going to brazen this thing out.

I thought of the dad I loved and the naked principal shaking the last drops of piss into our toilet, and I said something to Mom that I've regretted ever since: "Did you decide to abandon your husband the minute he was arrested or was it when they stripped him of his wealth?"

Mom calmly got a bowl out for the eggs. She broke the first egg to put in the bowl. Only she used an unusual technique; she smashed the egg with her open palm on the counter. She seemed quite pleased with the resultant egg mess on the counter and repeated the procedure. She smashed another egg after that. Then she picked up the carton and threw it on the floor. She stomped down with her left foot and then the right.

She raised her eyes to me and glared. I have never seen such anger in my mother's eyes, and I hope I never will again. "I wanted to 'abandon' that son of a bitch sixteen years ago when I discovered he was a liar and a cheat!"

She picked the carton up off the floor and began to smash it into the sink, presumably to make sure every egg was broken.

"I didn't do it then because of *you*! You have this blind spot when it comes to your dad. No matter how much trouble he gets into, you think the sun shines out of his ass. Well, let me tell you something, missy. He's good at playing the knight in shining armor, but in reality, he's no good!"

For a moment, I was looking at Linda Ronstadt, up on a stage, belting out: 'You're no good, you're no good; baby, you're no good." Then Mom stomped on one errant egg and marched off to her room.

I put a finger under one ear and drew it sharply across my throat. "Off with her head!"

We had agreed to play a set rather than a match. Three sets might have caused Cathy to break out in an unsightly sweat. And besides, high school kids don't have that long an attention span.

There was no point in me even trying to get into a fashion war with Cathy, so I just wore some cutoffs and a T-Shirt with a peace sign on it. I also wore my Air Jordan high-tops, which seemed to amuse the nouvelle richesse Cathy Anderson fans in their Reebok Pumps.

I had a small cheering section, which I hadn't expected. They were mostly hippies who had heard about the kegger Cathy was throwing after the match and feminists who had heard I was a lesbian. When we changed sides after the first game, my fans seemed kind of lifeless to me. The stoners were dozing off, and the girls were talking among themselves. I went over and led them in some cheers.

I waved my arms around and chanted, "Rah, Rah, Rizz, razz. Rich bitch girls can kiss my ass!"

It got my guys stoked up, but the upper crust seemed to find it in poor taste. They booed me. So I mooned them.

I went over to their section, turned my back to them, unzipped my cutoffs, pulled them down, and bent over.

The crowd went wild. There were nearly a hundred people there, and now eighty of them were yelling for me. I started to do it again, but Martha warned me that Coach Wilson was in the stands.

Cathy was pissed. When I charged the net for set point and then just tapped it an inch over the net, Cathy threw her racket at me. I ducked in time, but really, it was her best shot all day. I loved her at that moment. *Maybe*, I thought to myself, *she's not a mindless marionette after al*l.

If anyone thinks I took pity on the girl and let her win some games, you don't understand my competitive nature. Once the game has begun, I play to win. And I take no prisoners. When the set ended 6–0, we did take pity on her though. Martha brought out the sheets we had prepared. (I had uncharitably written USA–1, CSA–0 in large letters on the sheets.) I stood on Cathy's left; Martha stood on her right. We each held ends of the sheets—one in back, one in front. The sheets were an inch or so from her body, so she was technically naked. With nothing but her Confederate cap on, she walked back to the girl's dressing room.

When we got there, Cathy was handed a pile of her own clothes and announced she wanted to take a shower. I'd started to fall in line with the others exiting the dressing room, when Cathy took my hand and asked, "Would you stay?"

Yes, I would. I sat on a bench as she entered a shower stall. I watched her tennis outfit come flying out and splatter against the wall. Raising her voice enough to be heard over the cascading water, she asked me, "What did Stanley say to you?"

"What do you mean?"

"Please, Alys. Don't lie. I know he's talked to you, and I'm pretty sure what he asked. But I want to hear you say it."

What the hell? "He wants me to seduce you."

The sound of water stopped. Cathy appeared before me, stark naked. "Do you wish to begin now?"

Have you ever seen Botticelli's *The Birth of Venus*? You know, the one where she's standing in a seashell? That chick is not half as pretty as Cathy! I couldn't believe my eyes. I stood up and walked toward her. I grabbed a towel and wrapped it around her. I led her over to the bench and sat her down. I sat next to her.

"Now, what the hell's going on with you two? Are you his Trilby?"

"We're not lovers, Alys, if that's what you're thinking. We're more like brother and sister. I'm still a virgin, for your information."

"Cathy, I'm not thinking anything. The only things I know about you are that you're very beautiful and that you're a lousy tennis player."

Cathy made a little fist and punched my arm. (I'm never going to wash that arm.) "You're a brute," she said.

"I have to be honest with you, though. Stanley seems like a bit of a Svengali. You seem slavishly deferential to him."

"You don't understand, Alys. Stanley is super, super smart. He could be or do anything, but all he wants to do is make me happy."

"By making you a royal."

Cathy jumped back as if I had slapped her. "He told you that?"

"Well, yeah. But he swore me to secrecy."

"But you didn't keep the secret."

"I haven't told anybody."

"You just told me!"

"But you already knew."

"But you said you would keep it a secret!"

(*No, he's on third*, I thought to myself.)

"Cathy, listen. I will not tell anyone. If that's what you want in life, then I wish you the best of luck. I just wish you wouldn't let him control your every move."

"He's only trying to help."

"He tells me you are having feelings for women. He seems to think that, if we discreetly have sex, you'll get over these feelings. Apparently, he thinks I'm some sort of vaccine against homosexuality."

"I think he's right. You're such a horrible person, I think if I ate ice cream with you, I'd never want another spoonful of ice cream in my life."

"What's this? Cathy Anderson has a sense of humor?" I reached for her side to tickle her, and she froze.

"I'm sorry, Cathy. I invaded your private space. I don't do that. I was just playing."

"It's OK, Alys. We're just going to have to take this slow."

"Are we going through with this?"

"Yes, but on our own terms and at our own pace. Stanley is going to want to know every detail."

"Hey, Cathy. Do you want to have some fun?"

"Not tonight. I have a headache."

We both laughed. "No, but what I mean is, why don't you tell him we did it, and you love it? Tell him it's the best thing since sliced bread. Tell him, from now on, all you want is pussy!"

Cathy giggled. "I'm going to tell him it's the best thing since ice cream!"

That night I was tutoring Virgil on the Tudors. We were in my bedroom. My mom wants me to have a boyfriend so badly she lets us study with the door closed. After an hour or so, we put the books down and turned on the TV. We were on the bed, sitting up against the headboard, watching Johnny Carson. I felt totally relaxed, and during a commercial break, I went over to my closet. With just the open closet door between us, I removed my bra, so I'd be more comfortable. I came back to the bed in a good mood, and when Johnny cracked a particularly funny joke, I reached over to pat Virgil's leg the way people sometimes do when they are sharing a laugh.

For a second, I wondered what Virgil was doing with a roll of quarters in his pocket, and then he was all over me. He was grabbing me and kissing me with such passion that I feared it was a full-scale rape attack, and I panicked. I kneed him in the groin and smashed his nose with my elbow.

I jumped up and stood by the bed in a "strike" stance, left foot extended, my weight on the balls of my feet. Virgil rolled off the other side of the bed, groaning. He picked up the T-Shirt of mine with a peace symbol on it to staunch the flow of blood from his nose.

"What are you doing?" I asked.

"What am *I* doing? Psycho, what the fuck are *you* doing? What I was trying to do is called making love. What is wrong with you?"

"Virgil, I thought you understood. I'm a lesbian."

"You … oh my fuck." Virgil started laughing. Little bubbles of blood came out of his nostrils and popped. In a minute, he started crying. He stood and walked to the door.

"I'm so stupid," he said. "I'm so fucking stupid."

"Virgil."

"You will have to make your own way through the halls of Handley High," Virgil announced. "I can guide you no longer." With that, he was gone.

⌒〜〜

Here's my strategy when I play chess: Whenever you get the chance, kill somebody. My opponent invariably loses a lot of pawns, and I invariably lose the game. After three really quick games, Stanley stood up and said, "I have some business to take care of, Alys, but feel free to stay here as long as you want. Cathy will entertain you, somehow."

"He's very subtle, isn't he." Cathy laughed after he'd gone.

"At least he didn't say, 'there's a bed in that room, there.'"

"So, do I strip or what?"

I sighed. "Cathy, why don't we just talk? Come on, sit down. Get comfortable. It's just us girls here. Tell me what made you think you might be a lesbian."

Cathy took a long time to get started. I sensed she was running various explanations and scenarios through her head trying to come up with one that would best explain her feelings. I didn't rush her. "I don't fall asleep immediately," she began. "I lay in the bed awake for a long time. I think about things—things that happened that day, things I wonder about, feelings I have. Lately, I've thought about a girl I met recently. I can't stop thinking about her. Last month, I was thinking about her, and I … I touched myself."

That seemed to be all she could say. I had a lot of prurient questions (Was it me? Did you come?) But I didn't want to make her any more uncomfortable than she already was.

"Do you ever have those thoughts about boys?"

"No. I think a lot about my husband on my wedding day. I see myself walking down the hall in my beautiful wedding gown. It has …" (Here followed a ten-minute description of the glories of her wedding gown, all of which I blocked out.)

"I look towards the altar, and I see my husband. He's tall and handsome and wearing a bright, shiny suit. I can't see his face, but—"

"Let's get back to sex. I take it, when you see your husband, you don't touch yourself."

"*Ew*! Alys, don't be gross!"

"Cathy, I don't know what I'm going to do with you."

Stanley was pacing back and forth on the bleachers when I got there. "I said three o'clock!"

"Dude, I lost my guide, and I lost my way."

Stanley was not interested in my problems. "Man, what did you do to her? Are you some kind of sorceress? All she can talk about is pussy—pussy this and pussy that. What the hell have you done?"

"You told me to seduce her."

We were interrupted by noises from the tennis courts below. Three big guys in letter jackets were bothering Cathy and her singles partner. Stanley and I ran down there to check it out.

When we arrived, one of the thugs said, "Hey, Scovall, your girlfriend is looking good."

"Oh well. While Cathy is my oldest and dearest friend, I wouldn't really characterize her as—"

"Yeah, she looks good enough to eat," a pimply-faced smartass added. "I'd eat her," the third turd told us.

I recognized the leader of this motley crew. His name was Joe Scarvino. He desperately wanted to be known as Joe "the Scar" Scarvino, but he had no scar and most people referred to him as "Hey, you."

I walked up to him and I said, "Hey, you. I need you to muzzle your dog."

"Or what? What are you going to do about it, dyke?"

When two people are nose to nose, you can only exchange clever banter for so long before it becomes embarrassing for all concerned. There's time for talk and there's ... *Boom!*

Quicker than it takes to tell it, I grabbed his shoulders, put my right leg around his left, tripped him, and threw him into the post that holds up the net. Dazed, he managed to get up on his hands and knees, and I kicked him in the nose. Blood exploded everywhere.

I spun around to face the other two—and saw them walking away.

Next to me, Cathy's tennis partner was closing a switchblade. She slipped it into the pocket of her tennis outfit.

"Never leave home without it," she said with a big grin.

We turned and saw Cathy and Stanley scurrying in the direction opposite the way the thugs had left. "They're right, you know. The best thing they can do to help is get out of the way." The girl held out her hand. "Hi. I'm Starr, I'm named after a Beatle."

"Which one?"

Starr's black hair looked like it had been cut with hedge clippers. She stood five foot ten and she was skinny as a rail. I like a girl with skinny legs. Her breasts were the size of apples. I wanted to partake of that forbidden fruit. She had beautiful green eyes and a constant smile.

"Thanks for saving my ass," I said.

"De Nada," she replied, not so subtly checking out the aforementioned ass. "I've got to shower. Come with me and let's talk."

"Well, I don't know."

"I saved your ass, Loxley. Doesn't that rate a little talk?"

"How did you know my name?"

"If you hadn't had your head up Cathy's ass the last few weeks, you would know I've been stalking you."

"I'm flabbergasted."

"You're what?"

"It's something my grandmother says. It means astonished."

"I have that effect, sometimes."

Starr peeled her tennis outfit off as she went into the shower. I sat on a bench and looked around. Her backpack was partially opened, and I could see a paperback sticking out. I went over and pulled it out. *Tipping the Velvet* by Sarah Waters. It was a book I had read—several times, actually.

Starr came out of the shower, naked and dripping. It occurred to me that this was the second naked woman I'd seen in less than a week. She didn't make me think about Aphrodite.

She reminded me of a model and actress I had a prepubescent crush on called Twiggy. "How do you like the book?" I asked with forced casualness.

Starr's perennial smile dropped. "I'm at the part where Nan is aimlessly roaming the streets after Kitty's betrayal. I think it may be the saddest book I've ever read."

"I agree. But keep reading. Nan is tough and resilient. A broken heart may seem like the end of the world, but life goes on." (I was to remember those words, later.)

Starr seemed in no hurry to get dressed, and I nervously tried to make conversation.

"So, why have you been stalking me? Is it my breathtaking beauty? My incredible intellect? Perhaps, it's my humility."

Starr looked straight into my eyes and threw down the gauntlet. "It's your body. I want it."

I tried to maintain eye contact with her, but my body was on fire. Never had what I really wanted been offered to me so brazenly. I was afraid that … Well, that was it, wasn't it? I was afraid. If I professed my love for another girl, would I be publicly humiliated again? Like the most craven coward, I folded.

"Ha ha," I laughed, looking away. "My body! Yeah, right. That's really funny. Good one!"

When I got to government class, the teacher informed me that I was wanted in the principal's office. I was preoccupied with sixteenth-century cowards who had stood by in the face of Henry's evil and done nothing. When Henry condemned Thomas More to death for refusing to deny his Faith he had said, "*Off with his head!*" Why hadn't someone spoken up and said, "*No! Off with your head! Off with your head!*"?

I realized as I walked down the hall that I was actually muttering and making the sign for off with your head. I was unconsciously drawing a finger across my throat and whispering the words out loud. I looked up in embarrassment.

In front of me was the entire girls track team. They were giggling and pointing at me. Cathy was in the center of the group. Cathy's smile dissolved when she saw me, but she shrugged her shoulders and held her hands like Jesus in Raphael's *Transfiguration*, as if to say, "Hey, what can you do?"

And I had an epiphany. Yeah, I had me a fucking epiphany. Love and romance and all that shit belong in the supernatural realm. There is nothing rational about it. That fluttery feeling is just chemicals in your brain. Man ruts and vies for power like any other animal. That's it. That's the natural world. There's no such thing as love.

CHAPTER 6

WHAT WOULD LILITH DO?

I am never speaking to Cathy again after she laughed at me. Virgil won't speak to me after I humiliated him. Martha's new boyfriend doesn't like me. Martha says it's because I'm a Yankee, but I suspect it's because I'm a lesbian. Fuck 'em both. Fuck 'em all.

With Starr, I've turned into "the invisible woman." She won't acknowledge my existence. *God*! How I rue my cowardice. I wish I could go back to that moment when Starr said she wanted my body. I would do anything to be able to go back in time!

The little brunette came up to me and told me Coach wanted to see me.

"How many girls would you say Starr Williams has been with?" I asked her.

"I don't know about girls, but I heard she blew the entire Handley basketball team."

"That's bullshit."

"Yeah, it was probably just the starters."

"Sarah?"

The little brunette made herself scarce.

I thought about my new philosophy. Love is for suckers. Winning is everything. This was my creed from now on. I think that it's kinda cool and hip and fashionably cynical. Sort of like "and so it goes."

On the way to the gym, I ran into Starr. "I need to talk to you," I said.

"Can't. On my way to History. Ta."

"Hey, don't get your nose all out of joint just 'cause I left you with blue balls the other day. You need to know that somebody is spreading nasty lies about you. Just tell me who you want me to beat up."

Starr showed me that brilliant smile of hers. "You gonna defend my honor?"

I got down on one knee. Right there in the hallway of Handley High School. Kids stared and whispered. I didn't care. "I will defend your honor to the death," I vowed.

Starr laughed. "In that case, I guess I'm skipping history today."

When I told her what people were saying, Starr just shrugged it off. "That rumor," she said, "was started by Joe Scarvino last year.

He tried to grope me under the bleachers in the gym, and I had to dislocate his shoulder. He knew some of the guys on the basketball team, and they concocted some lurid tale of how they passed me around in the locker room."

"But you're gay. Who would believe such shit?"

"People believe what they want to believe."

"Yeah, I guess so. Virgil believed I was straight."

"And you're not?"

"You know I'm not."

Starr gave me that high-wattage smile of hers. "I would know, if you hadn't been such a pussy."

I asked Starr to come with me to the gym where Coach Rivers was in charge. I went up to Coach with a big smile of my own.

"Hi, Coach, did you want to see me?"

"Hi, Alys. No, I didn't send for you, but it's good to see you again. How's that thigh bruise?"

"It's a lot better, now, Coach."

A girl had fallen on my leg, going for a rebound, and Coach had rubbed some balm on my thigh for me. It felt good, but I'd begun to feel uncomfortable when her massage kept getting higher.

"That dumb Sarah said you wanted to see me."

"Maybe she meant Coach Wilson."

"OK. Bye." I turned and started running towards the coaches' offices.

"He's out on the football field," Coach Rivers called after me.

I stuck my left hand straight out like I was signaling for a left turn on a bike and ran out the door to the field. (What the hell? It got a few chuckles from the freshmen.)

Starr caught up to me. "Has she made a pass at you, yet?" she asked.

"Who, Coach? Are you nuts? She's nice."

"I bet she is. She couldn't take her eyes off your tits the whole time you were talking."

"Starr," I said (going for coquettish, and I'm sure, missing by a mile), "I think you're jealous!"

"Just leave that lady alone."

I was feeling pretty good when we got down to the football field. As we walked past the players practicing, I spotted Virgil. He was defending a receiver. The quarterback, Anthon Snowden threw a pass to Virgil's man. Just as he was about to try for an interception, I yelled, "Hi, Virgil!" as loud as I could.

The ball hit him in the face. The receiver grabbed him high, and another defender went low, hoping to catch the deflection. They split him in half.

As he lay moaning on the ground, I yelled at him, encouragingly, "Try to keep your eye on the ball, Virgil."

Starr stopped and stared at me like I was crazy. "What the fuck is wrong with you, Loxley?"

"Everybody hates me."

"Try a little tenderness."

"Eat me."

Coach Wilson was talking to an assistant when I walked up. I wasn't going to interrupt. I just stood there. After a couple of minutes, he finally looked at me and asked, "What do you want?"

"World peace."

Coach thought about that and then asked, "You Loxley?"

"Yes."

"Go to the office and have your sixth period changed to PE. Then report to the tennis courts. You're our new female tennis player."

"Sir, I don't like tennis."

"Do it for world peace, smart-ass."

⌁

The next time Lilith started nagging me about her church was soon after my conversation with Coach Wilson. His gag about world peace was still in my mind. I told her, "A church has to have a goal, like world peace, or at least some sort of redemption for its members. I see no socially redeeming value in your story at all. In fact, it seems completely pornographic. You get caught fucking a snake and get thrown out. You're replaced by Eve. End of story."

"No, no, no. I've told you already, the snake didn't do anything but accidentally trip Adam. And the story that I was too haughty for rutting is just one of Eve's lies. Write that down! Are you writing all this down?"

"I'll remember."

I didn't refuse to rut with Adam. I just thought it was fair that I should be on top sometimes. Eve took advantage of this. Adam would complain to her that my *pride* and *willfulness* were ruining the pleasure of the act for him. She indulged him. She got down on her hands and knees and let him take her the way he had seen the chimps do it. He would plow her from behind while she gasped, "Oh yeah, baby. Fuck my pussy! Fuck me good, Daddy."

When I confronted them with their vulgar behavior, they denied it!"

"Yeah?"

"Don't you see? I realized then that they had partaken of the forbidden fruit. They had tasted the fruit from the tree of the knowledge of good and evil. They began to cover themselves with fig leaves. They had turned reproduction into something to be ashamed of.

"So, your doctrine is what?"

"Truth, dumbass. The message of Lilith is *truth*."

<center>~~~</center>

Meanwhile, back at school, the center of the basketball team took a tumble down two flights of stairs. I thought Starr would be happy, but she acted like she was pissed at me. I tried playing the clown at tennis practice. I would pretend to lose her lobs in the sun and bounce them off my head, but she was not amused. Chasing a ball that was at least two feet out of bounds, I did a pratfall on a lawn chair. I got two scraped-up knees but no smile.

"What's the matter, Starr?"

"I can fight my own fights."

As she walked off in a huff, I thought of the kid's ditty that went, "Nobody likes me. Everybody hates me. Think I'll eat some worms.

The worms made me think of tequila, and tequila made me think of the time Coach Rivers had let me take a sip of her margarita at her apartment. Then, I thought about what Starr had said about Coach liking me. So, I went to Coach's apartment.

She was glad to see me. I was still in my tennis outfit, and Coach immediately noticed my scratched-up knees.

"Oh, my gosh. What happened? Come on in, and let's get those knees fixed up. Why didn't you go to the nurse's office?"

"Mrs. Turner is such a crab. I needed some TLC."

"Well, you came to the right place."

I ended up having dinner with Coach that night. Mom was out with Peterskin, so she didn't care. Coach wouldn't let me drink anything but Dr. Pepper, but every time she left the room, I topped it off with vodka. It wasn't too bad.

I ended up getting a little bit tipsy and started crying.

"What's the matter?"

I confessed to Coach that everybody hated me and life sucked. She came up with this Zen-like idea from out of the blue. "Why don't you forget about yourself and do something to make someone else happy?"

"But I don't know any poor people."

"Get Martha Mendoza to help you."

It was a brilliant idea, and I was beginning to feel good for the first time in a while. I jumped up and gave Coach a kiss.

At that moment, I began to feel the power that Lilith had given me. I knew that under different circumstances Marjorie Rivers and

I could have made hot, blissful, mad love at that moment. We could have driven each other to heretofore unknown heights of bliss.

"Alys, you should go."

I stopped on the porch. "Coach, if I ever win at Wimbledon, I'm going to bring you the Rosewater Dish." And I meant it.

CHAPTER 7

THANKSGIVING 1987

"Hi, Martha. I'm glad I caught you by yourself so I can hug you and wish you a happy Thanksgiving without upsetting Estaban."

"Forget Estaban. I dumped him last weekend. My new guy is Freddy. He doesn't care if you're gay as long as you don't drive a Ford. He's a Chevy guy."

"Cool. So, maybe you could help me with something. I've been depressed lately. All my friends except you are treating me really shitty. Coach Rivers said I should help some less fortunate souls, so I'll feel better about myself. I figured you know some poor Mexicans who could use some canned goods."

"So, the whole purpose of this charitable endeavor is to make you feel better?"

"Yeah. What else?"

Suddenly, Martha was center stage with the spotlight on her. She wore a glittery dress and was backed up by Three Dog Night. They were singing their hit song, "Easy to be Hard."

Martha sang, "Do you only care about the bleeding crowd? How about a needy friend? We all need a friend."

Martha spoke a little louder since I wasn't responding. "You're going to give food to a Mexican on a family holiday? Estupida! A Mexican may not have anything else, but she always has family. Why don't you have an orphan over to your house for Thanksgiving dinner?"

"Where am I going to find an orphan?"

"What about your fuckbuddy, Starr?"

"Starr's an orphan?"

"Alys, you amaze me. You may not be the most self-absorbed person in the world, but you're right up there at the top."

"Besides, we're not fuck buddies. Not yet. I kinda chickened out when I had the chance."

"*What*? Chica, I don't mind you being gay, but don't be a pussy! Do you want to be a virgin forever?"

"I almost lost it Friday night, but not to Starr."

"Dios mio, not Coach Rivers. I'm telling you, Chica, leave that poor woman alone.

So, I ended up asking Starr over for Thanksgiving. She told me she might drop by if she had time.

At ten o'clock on Thanksgiving Day, the doorbell rang. I answered it. A beautiful, squeaky-clean girl in a white dress stood there holding a Kroger pecan pie. It was Starr, of course, but I almost didn't recognize her. I'd never seen her in a dress, but that wasn't the only thing. Her wild, tangled black hair had been tamed and held in place with some kind of gel. She had on some cheap earrings and just a touch of makeup.

I smiled.

Before I could say anything, Starr said, "Don't you dare laugh, Loxley."

"No, no. You look great." I looked for a car leaving, but I didn't see one. It turned out her Uncle Rick had dropped her at the Handley Road exit off the freeway. She'd walked five blocks to get here.

Martha had been surprised that I didn't know Starr was a foster child living with the Hernandezes. The fact is I'm not good with intimacy. If I'm curious about someone else's personal life, they are inevitably going to show an interest in mine. And that's something I do not wish to share.

Mom loved Starr immediately. The only other friend of mine she knew was Martha, and Mom considered her to be a "bit of a tart." She knew she was going to like Starr, she said, "because Ringo is my favorite Beatle."

Mom never has more than a glass of wine with dinner during the week, but during football season, Sundays are different. Fran Loxley drinks Budweiser on Sundays during football season. She drinks a prodigious amount. She opens her first beer during the kickoff of the first game at noon and is never without a beer in her hand the rest of the day.

After a huge meal and assorted pies and cakes for dessert, there was still more than an hour before the Cowboy kickoff. We sat in the living room, our bellies full.

"How is it," my mom asked, "that you go to Handley, when the Hernandezes live on the North Side?"

I was surprised when I heard the question. It said a lot about my mother (or about me) that she had known this girl less than four hours, and she knew where she lived and with whom.

"I used to go to Carter/Riverside. I went to the football game when Carter/Riverside went to Handley's stadium. I watched the cheerleaders doing their dazzling routine in their beautiful outfits and I said, 'That's for me.'"

I wish I had known then that one of those cheerleaders (the one Starr was watching) was Cathy Anderson.

"Felix and Belinda's oldest girl had a job working in the Handley cafeteria. She was able to get an apartment near the school. I used her address to transfer to Handley."

"Do you actually live there with her?" Mom asked her.

"Sometimes. I move around a lot. I stay with her, Inez, a lot. Sometimes I go home to the Hernandezes. Who knows? Maybe I'll move in here?"

Mom laughed. "Oh, wouldn't that be lovely. You're welcome over here, any time."

I stared at Starr in amazement. She had totally won over my mom.

Mom said, "Tell me about Denver."

"Well, Felix worked at the Coors brewery, and Belinda cleaned houses. I had a foster brother and two foster sisters, plus Felix and Belinda's own kids, Inez and Carlos. It was a big, happy family. Not all foster families are miserable, you know. Then Felix was offered a foreman's job at the new Miller brewery on the South freeway, and we moved down here."

"Oops," Mom said and made a big production of hiding her Bud Light can. The game hadn't even started yet, and she was already getting tipsy. "What about your parents? Do you remember anything about them?"

"Mo-om!" It seemed to me she was getting too personal now.

"It's OK," Starr said. "I don't remember much about them. My mom died when I was eight, and I've been in foster care ever since. The nearest I've ever had to family was my Aunt Helen. She wasn't my actual aunt; she was just a friend of my mom's. She and her little girl used to visit me two or three times a year."

Mom was unusually quiet after that. Once, when she was returning from the kitchen with a fresh beer, I heard her mumble, "Her name was Helen?" but Starr didn't hear her. A minute later, the Cowboys took the field.

"Hey, look," Mom yelled, "There's Danny White. Hey, Danny! Try to throw it to the guys with the star on their helmets."

Starr and I decided to go up to my room.

I sat on my bed while Starr took a seat at my vanity table.

"Starr," I said, "Martha has recently chided me for knowing virtually nothing about you. You've always seemed rather reserved about your past, but I desperately want to be your friend, Starr. Do you want to tell me anything about you?"

Starr looked at me with her mesmerizing green eyes. "Do you want to know me, Alys? Do you want to know me intimately?"

"Yes, Starr. Please."

"If we do this thing, you must keep my secret—"

"I promise I'll—"

"Shut up! I'm a dom, Alys. I can only enjoy sex with a partner who is completely submissive to me. Will you do anything I say?"

"Uh … well, you know. When you say anything …"

Starr laughed. "Geez, Alys, you just ruined the whole game. Do you have to be so literal? Come here." She started undressing me. "Alys, honey, you don't even know it, yet, but you're a submissive. You will enjoy this experience a whole lot more if you don't have to worry about what to do. Just relax and let me take control. Don't be afraid. Nothing painful or sick is going to happen. I would never do anything you didn't want me to do. You must know that."

And I did. And what happened after that was the most beautiful, most joyous experience I've ever experienced. I cried tears of joy as Starr screamed in ecstasy at my ministrations.

From downstairs, Mom yelled, "That was the Vikings that scored, ya moron!"

⌒⌒

On Saturday night, about eleven o'clock, the doorbell rang. Mom was out on a date with Peterskin. Grandmother had long since gone to bed for the night. I was in bed reading an Ed McBain 87th Precinct novel. I got up and went downstairs. When I opened the door, a very drunk Virgil Wilder threw my peace T-shirt in my face.

"I couldn't get the blood stains out," he said.

"That's all right," I told him. "You didn't have to return it."

"Oh, I *wanted* to return it," he assured me. "I wanted to return it. You know why? I wanted to return it because …" It took him a moment, but he remembered. "I wanted to return it because I don't want *anything* from a manipulative, cold-blooded prick-teaser like you!"

The teddy I wear to bed is sheer, almost transparent. Virgil was staring at my breasts. "I can see the darkness of your oreolies," he told me.

"Are you saying 'areolas'?

"Don't be such a smart-ass, Loxley. Do you think you're smarter than me? Do you think you are better than me? Do you think you're too good for a guy from Texas?" He almost fell off the porch at that point.

"Do you need me to drive you home?"

"Ha! You're prakally naked! I can see the darkness of your oreos. Why can't I see the darkness down there where your pubic hair is?"

"Starr makes me shave," I replied, matter-of-factly.

He lunged at me, but I was ready. I put my foot out, grabbed his shoulders, rolled backwards, and used the impetus of his charge to throw him into the wall behind me. I put him in a choke hold, and I told him, "Never try that again. The last man who tried that is dead."

I tossed him out into my yard. I wasn't sorry I had hurt him, but I did wish I hadn't said that last bit.

CHAPTER 8

TWO TRAGEDIES

I was lying on my bed staring at the ceiling when I was attacked. My attacker jumped on top of me demanding, "Your gold or your virtue, mate."

"You'll never get my gold, you blasted pirate." I giggled. "But if you can find me virtue, it's yours."

Starr and I rolled around and tickled for a while, but she could sense something was wrong. She rolled off me and laid a hand gently on my stomach. "What's wrong, puss?"

"A long time ago, my mom told me some shit about my dad. I thought it was just her guilty conscience because I had caught her doing Mr. Peterskin, the principal."

"Ew."

"Yeah, it was pretty gross. Anyway, I got to wondering if any of it could be true, and I decided to write to Dad. Today, I got a reply.

"What did he say?"

"I haven't read it, yet."

"Give it to me. I'll read it."

I pushed the letter down under my butt. "I'm not ready, yet."

Starr stood up and paced the floor for a while.

"If you don't mind me asking, what did your mom say?" Starr asked.

"She said that Dad messed around on her and got a woman pregnant. This was while Mom was pregnant with me. She claims that Dad was going to leave us for this other woman but that he got arrested, and she wouldn't wait for him. She married someone else, even though she was pregnant with Dad's baby."

"Did she what the other woman's name was?"

"Mom called her 'Hell on Wheels.' I don't know her real name."

"Helen Wheeler."

"What?"

"Alys, I think before you read that letter, it's time for me to tell you about my past.

My mom killed herself when I was eight. I found her slumped over the kitchen table, an empty bottle of pills and an almost empty bottle of whiskey next to her. When I couldn't get her to wake up, I tried to dial 9-1-1, but our phone was disconnected. I went out and tried to find a neighbor who would help, but my mom was widely disliked by everyone. She was a nymphomaniac and an alcoholic. Some said she was a whore. But if she'd charged for it, it seems we could have paid our phone bill. Eventually, I had to walk five blocks to the fire station before I could get help.

"A few hours later, my Aunt Helen showed up. That's who she told me she was. I didn't know her. I was in shock anyway. Aunt Helen took me to her husband, Jerry Dunnally, and tried to get him to take me in since he was my biological father. He refused. He said he had thrown my mother out before I was born and would have nothing to do with me.

Although she had to turn me over to foster care, Helen came to visit me whenever she got the chance. She always brought her daughter, Amy. Amy and I got to know each other. She was a strange child. It was she who told me that Scott Loxley was her real father. She had the crazy idea that you were her evil stepsister who stole her daddy away from her.

"I have a sister?" I asked.

"Helen admits that Scott Loxley was the father of Amy. She says there was no deception. She admitted to Jerry that she was already pregnant when they met. He apparently loved her so much he didn't care. Although, that makes you her half-sister rather than stepsister."

"Still, that's half a sister more than I knew about before." I lay there thinking about my (now extended) family. Did my mom know Helen? How good of friends were Helen and Starr's mom?

Suddenly, the covers were ripped off the bed. Starr stood over me and, in her best Captain Cook imitation, said, "Madam, I have lost a very valuable treasure map, and I have reason to believe you are cognizant of its whereabouts!"

"But, good sir, I am but an innocent, young girl. What would I know of treasure maps?"

"I don't believe you, wench. I think you've hidden my prize in some secret place, and I intend to search you until I find it."

"Fine, just don't shiver me timbers."

<hr />

"Thank you," I said later.

She hugged me and kissed my cheek. "You OK now?"

"Yes, and I'm ready to open that letter, now."

"Do you want some privacy?"

"No, Starr. Please stay. I need you here."

The letter from Dad had ended up on the floor. It was quite crumpled. I opened it up and read:

Dear Princess,

Thanks for writing to me. Getting mail is the high point of my day. I wish the subject matter had been something lighter. Frankly, I can't believe your mother would air our dirty laundry in front of you. You must have really pissed her off (or she was really drunk).

Your tone was strident. No less than three times, you demanded "the truth." Well, your eighteenth birthday is just right around the corner, and I suppose you are old enough for the truth.

It's kind of sad, though. I remember reading you tales of knights on quests and princesses who just knew their hero would rescue them. You never demanded "the truth" back then, and you always went to sleep happy. So, here's the truth, honey.

Your mother married me to get out of Fort Worth and live a life of wealth and glamour. She was always complaining that I wasn't making enough money. She never loved me for myself.

Then I met Helen. We fell deeply and truly in love. It's true that Helen and I conceived another child while you were still in the womb. The truth is, hon, if I had my choice, I would have gone to live with them. Circumstances interfered and I stayed in a loveless marriage. I did it for you. I'm sorry that in "real life," we don't all "live happily ever after."

Love,
Your dad

P.S. If you finish that novel you're writing, let me see it. There are a lot of literary agents and editors here in prison.

"Wow, your dad is … quite a guy.

"Fuck you, Starr. You know he was arrested, and Helen moved on. God! She moved on to *your* biological father. This whole thing is so freaking incestuous! And he never even mentioned Amy."

"He probably forgot about her."

"Well, that's it then. He is not getting a card on Father's Day."

～✗～

Once I began avoiding both Cathy and him, Stanley decided Cathy needed a high-profile boyfriend to quash the rumors that she liked girls. Stanley chose Anthony Snowden as Cathy's next boyfriend. Anthony had been voted "Most Likely to Own Fort Worth." His family was richer than the Basses.

Stanley didn't bother conferring with Anthony or Cathy. He went straight to the highest authority to arrange this match. He met with Mrs. Phyllis Berkley-Snowden and told her frankly, though reluctantly, that her only son was whoring around with the lower classes."

"He needs a good, clean girl with a respectable pedigree," Stanley told her, "a girl like Cathy Anderson."

So, without ever even meeting, Anthony Snowden and Cathy Anderson became the most popular couple at Handley High School. This mirrors, almost exactly, the engagement between Henry VIII and Anne of Cleves.

And we all know how that turned out.

～✗～

When school let out for the holidays, we were still debating whether or not to take the "Bianca Delgado Case." That, and a good name for our gang of vigilantes were the main topics of conversation when we got together on those cold days before Christmas. (When I say cold, I mean upper forties to low fifties for a high and around freezing for a low.)

I wanted to call the group Teenage Lesbian Ninja Vigilantes. Everybody laughed at me.

We settled on Vaginal Vigilantes, although I didn't really like it. It made it sound like we rounded up deadbeat pussies to me.

Bianca was a friend of Martha's who had come to us for muscle. "I want to order a hit," she said.

"If you want him dead, it's extra," Starr deadpanned.

Bianca stared at her for a second and then said, "Fuck you." Turning to me, she said, "Tell your lesbian lackey I don't want anything to happen to the guy who gave me this black eye. I want y'all to help me hurt the girl who made him do it."

"Who might that be?" I asked.

"Names Cathy Anderson."

We stared at Bianca.

"Blonde girl?" Starr asked. "Blue eyes? About yay high?"

Having confirmed the identity of the suspect, Starr homed in on the pertinent details of the case.

"But she didn't actually hit you, right?"

"No. See, I've been dating this guy. Real classy. Nice dresser."

"Rich," Martha noted.

"Course," Bianca replied. "He would take me shopping and buy me some nice things. Then, we would go to a hotel. It was nice. It went on for a few months, and then, suddenly, no Tony. No calls. No nothing. So, one day I see him at school and I'm like, 'What the fuck?' you know? He tells me he's found this rich bitch he's trying to get in good with."

"'Nothing personal, baby doll,' he says. 'But she's almost as rich as I am, and Mom says we make a real cute couple.'"

"Really cute," Martha corrected.

"Well, not to me," Bianca insisted, "I don't think they are a cute couple at all. It pisses me off when his mom tells him he can only date girls 'of his own class.' The Delgados got more class than anyone else on the North Side. My dad owns two pawn shops. I told him, 'Chinga su madre.' But he just shrugged it off. It wasn't until I keyed his Camaro that he does this." She pointed to her eye.

"You keyed his Camaro?" Starr gasped, aghast. "Your Honor, a clear case of justifiable assault if I ever did see one."

Bianca looked at me with an exaggerated expression of patience. "I already told your boy toy over here, I got no beef with Tony. I just want you to rough up the stuck-up bitch that took him away from me."

"We sort of specialize in bullies," I said.

Then Martha spoke up: "Boss, just think of boyfriends as lunch money. A bully can steal lunch money because he's bigger and stronger than the victim. Girls like Cathy can steal boyfriends because they're rich, pretty, and their shit don't stink. Same, same."

"She's got a point," Starr admitted.

"You think so, Toy?" I asked, coyly.

"Don't make me come over there," she replied with that big grin of hers.

"Hey! You two take a cold shower," Bianca yelled. "Are you going to help me or not?"

～✻～

I was cooking dinner that night. Mom was on a date, and Grandmother was upstairs in her room watching *NCIS*. Starr was on the living room couch watching *That Girl*. She was wearing men's boxers and a sports bra. She looked adorable. She was talking to me about our newest client, Bianca Delgado. She was saying that she thought Bianca was a bit of a whore.

I was thinking that any interaction between men and women was transactional. Men always want something. Mainly, they want one thing.

And when they get it, they think they own you. If you "surrender" your virginity to them, you're "used" merchandise. Women are a commodity to men; and they like to keep us servile. Men don't hold doors open for women because they don't think women are capable of opening doors. They do it to keep women in a constant state of dependence and gratitude.

I realized I was slipping into my dark place.

Men have no conception of love, I said to myself. *They know only self-gratification.* "The only reason men do *anything*," I said, suddenly speaking out loud, "is so they can fuck you!" I threw the spatula I was holding into the sink. I gripped the edge of the countertop with shaking hands, and I fought to hold back the tears.

Then I felt Starr's hands on my shoulders. "Honey, you're burning the Hamburger Helper."

She helped me make dinner and we ate it in front of the TV.

I should have told her then. I should have told her everything. If I had told her about the things that happened when I was fifteen, things might have turned out differently. I just couldn't do it. That horror was buried. I couldn't disinter that ugliness. But I vowed to never be a downer around Starr again. I was going to be upbeat and happy and fun to be around. And most importantly, I was going to keep her the most satisfied sexual partner in the world.

To that end: "Starr, I'm sorry I spazzed out earlier. It won't happen again. I'm feeling better now. How about you? Are your legs cramping? Why don't you let me take a look?" I knelt in front of her and began to knead her thighs. I grabbed some moisturizer and applied it to both legs. I rubbed it all the way down her right leg to the foot and all the way back up the left to her boxers. Starr spread her legs to facilitate my massage.

Those damn boxers! They don't cover anything!

We heard the doorbell, but we were busy. Eventually, we answered it.

"It's about time," Martha complained, "I've been knocking on this door for five minutes."

"We were coming as fast as we could," Starr answered, and then burst into uncontrollable laughter.

Martha wanted to bring me up to date on Bianca's case. We had decided that we were not the kind of gang that went around beating people up. (*She* decided that. I went along with it.) We didn't believe in "a black eye for a black eye." Bianca had reluctantly agreed to accept "public shaming" as an appropriate punishment.

Martha, Bianca, Starr, and I had attended the Winter Dance. Just as Cathy was about to be crowned Ice Queen, Martha yelled, "We would like to ask you a question."

"Anything you say will be held against you," Starr added. "Why did you tell 'Asshat' Anthony to hit Bianca?" I asked.

"Don't be ridiculous. *If* Anthony hit her, it's because she wouldn't stop stalking him. If he hit her, it was, no doubt, self-defense. She's a violent little trollop with no breeding. Anthony does not know her. He looked me right in the eye and said, "I did not have sex with that woman."

"Why is your boyfriend quoting the president of the United States?" Martha (along with other inquiring minds) wanted to know.

"A sign of the times?" Cathy answered. "I don't know. All I know is that there *is* not and *never has been* a relationship between my Anthony and that nobody."

Witnesses say that, at that point, Bianca began laughing. "You've never been naked with him!" she crowed. "Hey, if he ever does decide he wants to do you, check out the tattoo on his inner thigh. If he doesn't want me, why does it say 'Bianca' next to his dick?"

"We rest our case," Starr said.

My holiday break was idyllic. Starr and I seldom left my bedroom. When we did, Mom or Grandmother would have cookies or cakes in the oven. I could almost have been convinced that God was in Her heaven and all was right with the world—until I was visited by the Ghost of Past Horrors.

The phone rang at 3:05 a.m., January 1, 1987.

"I'm done," a very hoarse voice whispered. "I'm out. Call it off." I recognized the voice of Bianca Delgado.

"Where are you?" I asked, "Are you hurt?"

There was a snort on the line and Bianca said, "Yeah, you could say that. I got two busted ribs and a busted finger. My face looks like a jack-o'-lantern that was dropped from a roof.

"And … they …" Bianca started to sob. "I tried to fight back, Alys. I promise. I'm just not as strong as you."

"Bianca, just tell me where you are. Do you need me to take you to the hospital?"

"I just left there, Alys. I'm home now. I only called you to let you know I'm out of this shit. I don't want Anthony back. She can have him. I quit."

"Bianca, may I come over to your place?"

"It won't do you any good. I'm not changing my mind. It's not worth it. No man is. I tried to fight, Alys. There were two of the bastards. They both—"

"I'm coming to your house." I found her address and took a taxi. I told her mother I was a close friend. She acted skeptical, but she let me in.

I held Bianca all night. I told her what had happened to me. We cried together. We talked about the fear that all women have at one time or another—the existential fear of being a weak, soft creature in a world of mean brutes. I promised Bianca, "This will not stand. I will deal with this." I took her hands in mine—hands bruised from trying to defend herself from animals.

"Don't kill them," Bianca said to me when I left at dawn. "Just make them feel like I did when they raped me."

CHAPTER 9

MEA CULPA, MEA CULPA, MEA MAXIMA CULPA

"Fuck her if she can't take a joke."

This was Martha's take on the fight I was having with Starr. We were at her house getting ready for a party that Cathy was throwing in my honor. I was district champion in female singles tennis. I had just been ranked fourteenth in the state. I'm not saying that Cathy and I were on good terms now, but Cathy never needed much of an excuse to throw a party.

I watched the half-dressed Martha applying makeup in front of her mirror. Since leaving my upper-crust upbringing in New York, I have strived to be egalitarian. But it was difficult for me to see how there could be so much beauty in such a simple girl. Martha has had dozens of boyfriends since I've known her. They all seem the same to me. They all have greasy hair and dirt under their fingernails. They all work at garages and drive a Chevy pickup truck. And yet this *Venus*, this *Aphrodite*, would scratch a waitress's eyes out for flirting with one of them. Those rednecks don't deserve her!

And, I think she had the right take on this thing. It was Starr who was in the wrong, not me.

I had sat down hours ago to sort things out. I fixed myself a cranberry vodka and weighed the pros and cons of our relationship. I decided to speak out loud for the sake of clarity.

"Pro," I said, like a lawyer in court, "we are fabulous in bed.

"Con, Starr has cut me off. Since the silly misunderstanding with Candi, she won't let me touch her."

"What silly misunderstanding?"

"*Fuck*! Would you not do that? Can't you announce your presence before you start speaking to me?"

"I suppose I could blink the lights in the room on and off when I arrive. Would that help?"

"I don't know, but let's try it. Anyway, it was nothing. I was proselytizing to the cheerleaders in your name—"

"You were trying to get laid."

"Whatever. When I was leaving, Candi caught up to me under the bleachers. She told me she was becoming confused about her sexuality, so I told her of a simple test. Get a picture of a naked woman and another of a naked man. When you masturbate that night, see which picture you're looking at.

"She told me then that she hadn't been able to stop thinking of my tits when she masturbated. 'Do you think I might get just a glimpse of them?' she asked me.

"Well, what could I do? As soon as I removed my bra, she *had* to touch them. Then, of course, she needed to kiss and lick them. At that point, it occurred to me that the 'acid test' would be if she were wet at that moment. So, I reached my hand down inside her little cheerleader outfit.

"Well, you could have knocked me over with a pom-pom if Starr didn't show up right then. Some coincidence, huh?"

"You? You are the rock upon which I will build my church? Fuck me."

Lilith didn't seem to want to talk anymore, so I fixed myself another drink and continued my list.

Con, like so many uneducated girls, Starr confuses "love" with "possessiveness." I love you; therefore, you are mine. I love you the way I love my favorite show horse or my favorite car.

I don't know if you like cranberries, but I find them tart and sweet at the same time. Vodka just seems to add a little something to that flavor. Let's see.

Con, she sulks a lot. I don't like it when people bring me down. She should be thanking her lucky stars she has me … But, I mean, she doesn't have me. I don't belong to anyone!

Ahh, the clarity that comes with the fifth cranberry vodka. I found Starr in Mom's driveway throwing a tennis ball against the garage door. I had lost my pro/con list, but I remembered the important thing.

"I don't belong to anyone!" I don't think I slurred any words, but the effect was minimalized by the slight swaying of my body.

Starr bounced the tennis ball a few times. Then she looked at me sadly and said, "I know you don't, baby. And you don't know the slightest thing about love."

"Pfft," I said. "I am the greatest lover since Casanova!"

I've seen Starr go into "berserker" mode when we were outnumbered in a fight. It was a frightening sight, even when you were on her side. Now the madness possessed her. She dropped the ball and grabbed my shirt with both hands and pulled me to her.

"Go to your fucking victory party and hoity-toity with the highfalutin hos. I'll be cruising gay bars and picking up chicks. I'm going to drink till I puke and have lots of hot sex with strangers. All the things you think are so great, *I'll* be doing tonight!"

She shoved me away and I landed in a nearby hedge.

"I hate you!" I thought I heard her exclaim as she walked away.

Then she was suddenly standing over me. She was icy calm. She slowly dissolved. Her brightly colored individual cells danced around and rearranged themselves into Linda Ronstadt. "I broke a heart," she sang, "that was gentle and true. I broke her heart over someone like you. I'll beg her forgiveness over bended knee. I wouldn't blame her if she said to me. 'You're no good. You're no good. You're no fucking gooood.'" And she was gone.

She was right, of course. Still.

"Martha, do you think there could be something wrong with Starr? I've never seen her like she was just now. She's never been violent with me before. Her eyes were all crazy. I wonder if it could be something hereditary. You know her mom was a suicide, and her father never acknowledged her as his daughter."

"It could be, Alys, that she has developed 'trust issues.'"

"So, what crawled up her ass all of a sudden?"

Martha looked at me sadly and said, "Honey, if you don't know, I can't explain it."

"It's like that old song," I explained to the little brunette girl, "you know?

"'You don't own me, dum de du da da dum … And when you go out with me, don't put me on display.' You know? Thish iz wat I wuz trying to splain to her.

"So, what else could I do, Sarah?"

"You remembered my name."

"That's exactly right. If she hadn't gone off in a huff, we could have talked things over, but she didn't, did she? I mean she did. She just turned her pretty head and walked away."

I tipped my metaphorical hat to the James Gang and did a little drum riff on the coffee table. The little brunette made herself scarce.

"Is there any more vodka?" I yelled. "What? *That's* vodka? How long have I been holding that?"

Suddenly, I was looking at the (perfectly composed) face of Cathy Anderson.

"Hello, come here often? Ha ha. Get it? It's your house and I asked you …"

"It looks like you and Sarah were having an interesting conversation."

"Who's Sarah?"

"You better come with me, dear." Cathy took me to the kitchen. "Here. Drink some water."

Cathy is soooooooo nice. She has really good water! "Hey, I remember what she said."

"You want another sip?"

"She said I could 'hoity-toity' all I wanted with the Country Club Cunts."

"Are you sure she didn't say something about the hoi polloi?"

"She told me you're not nearly as tough as you think you are."

"She's tough enough for all of us."

"I think she loves another."

"You may need to lie down."

"I love you."

Looking back, I think Cathy intended to reach under my arm and lift me. I think she was going to put me to bed so I could sober up. But at the time, I thought she was coming in for a kiss. I grabbed her and forced my slack, slobbery lips to hers. She jerked her head back and pushed me away with revulsion. I fell to my knees and, looking past Cathy, saw Starr. I fell to the floor, sobbing. I couldn't seem to stop.

THE HIDDEN CHAPTER YOU MUSTN'T TELL ALYS ABOUT

Starr and Cathy stood over the inert body of Alys Loxley. "I'm sorry you had to see this," Cathy sighed.

"Don't say, 'I told you so.'" Starr said. "I knew she was just pissed at you when she took me for a lover. I just … well, fuck it. What are we going to do about this?" She indicated the star athlete at their feet who had chosen to wear a bloodstained T-shirt with a peace sign on it, a fluffy ballerina-style skirt, and some scuffed Doc Martens to a party held in her honor.

"Do you think we can get her upstairs to my bedroom?"

With one of her arms around each of their necks, they managed to coax the extremely limp and increasingly heavy body up the stairs.

"Come on, baby. You can do it." "That's right. Now the other foot."

At one point, Alys stopped, stood very straight, and said with exaggerated dignity, "Free Bird." Then she sank back into inebriation and crapulence. They got her Doc Martens off. They were going to relieve her of the silly ballerina thing but stopped and rolled their eyes when they discovered that it was crotchless and she wore no panties. They left it on her and covered her with a sheet.

They sat on the other side of Cathy's enormous bed. They each had a lot to say but were worried about the other one's reaction.

"When did you fall in love with Alys?" Cathy asked.

"The first time she made me orgasm," Starr admitted.

"It wasn't love at first sight then?"

"Not love. Interest to the point of obsession but not love. I knew I had to get to know her. She fascinated me. My friend, Amy, had told me about her. Amy doesn't know her. She's never met her, but she's heard about her since she was a baby. Alys is the evil princess who cast a spell over their father and took him away from Amy.

Starr said, "I followed Alys around while she pursued you. I discovered that she had once been a 1 percenter. She wasn't pretty and popular like you, though. She discovered last year that the only thing that held her in the upper class was her father's money. It was suddenly gone, and she found herself trapped in the middle class. Subconsciously, she saw you as an escape. Consciously, well, she's a lesbian, and you're the prettiest girl in the school. Nothing more to say."

"Stanley asked her to seduce me."

"I know."

"I came to you then."

"Don't remind me."

"I told you then that, ever since you rescued me on the tennis court, I've been having fantasies about you. I begged you then. I said, 'Stanley is going to force me to have sex with another girl anyway. Why shouldn't it be with someone I love? I told Alys that I had been fantasizing about a girl, and she naturally assumed I meant her, but it was you. And you told me you couldn't be unfaithful to Alys."

"I feel pretty stupid, now."

REDUX

I woke up on Martha's couch. I don't know how I got there. I had a terrible headache. I couldn't remember much. Everything was hazy.

The bits I could remember were nightmarish. What possessed me to drink in the afternoon? Why had I gone to that stupid party? What had *happened* at that party?

I couldn't find my keys. I couldn't find my phone. I felt a paralyzing sense of dread. Something was wrong! Someone was trying to convince someone: "Nothing happened. Nothing happened. Nothing happened."

I prayed to Saint Agnes, "Forgive me for whatever I did last night. Make it not have happened." (I don't believe in God, but when I'm really frightened, I pray to St. Agnes, the Patron Saint of Rape Victims and Virgins.) Even as I stumbled over the grammatical clumsiness of that sentence the answer came to me: "Sorry. Once something has happened, it cannot be undone." I guess that applies to whatever happened last night.

I ran out of Martha's place and almost knocked her down on her front porch.

"Hey, Martha. I want to ask you how I got here last night, but I gotta run right now. I have to get home and apologize to Starr for going to that stupid party last night."

"She's gone."

"She … wait, what?"

"She's gone, and she's not coming back. You will never see her again. She told me to give you this."

Martha handed me an envelope with my name on it. I recognized Starr's handwriting.

"She got a call last night telling her to go to the party," Martha told me. "When she got there, she saw you kissing Cathy.

"You disgusting turd," she added.

I stood there on Martha's porch and felt my life come to an end.

CHAPTER 10
PENANCE: SUMMER OF 1987

I took the crumpled letter from my pocket and read it for the twentieth time. Like Lady McBeth compulsively washing her hands, I could not make what it said go away.

Alys,

I remember how nervous you were when we first made love. You were like a little schoolgirl taking an important test. You were terribly frightened that you would make an error and fail the test. You were so innocent that day. I can't help but think that I took away your purity that day. You were so proud when I orgasmed. I thought you were going to run down the street yelling, "I got an A. I got an A."

You're very competitive, my little cherub. You want to be the youngest author to have a best seller. You want to be a hero and vanquish injustice. And you want to be a lesbian lothario. I'm very afraid that you see lovemaking as a skill and hope to be "the best ever."

I suspect you have secrets. I think that's why you fear intimacy. The many ways you hurt me when we were together may have been your way to keep me at arm's length. I can tell you this, my little kitten; without intimacy you'll never know love. If you're not careful, you'll end up just like your *father*.

You will never know how you've hurt me. You ripped my heart right out of me and left me unable to love. There is another pure girl who wanted to give me her love, but you ruined that. For stealing my ability to trust and love, I curse you. Damn you to hell, Alys Loxley!

Fuck a porcupine,

Starr Williams

P.S. Don't try to find me. You are dead to me. If I
ever see you again, *beware*. I'll be armed.

I got drunk and stayed drunk for about a week. Then one day,
I woke up and found a guy rummaging through Starr's stuff in my
room. I noticed Martha standing just inside the door.

"Take it easy, Alys," she said. "I'm here for his protection as
much as yours."

"Who are you and why are you messing with Starr's stuff?" I
asked the stranger.

"My name is Sam Dunnally. I'm Starr's brother. She asked me
to get some of the stuff she couldn't carry with her when she came
home."

"Home?"

"Yeah, Starr has moved back to Denver. She lives with my
stepsister, Amy. Mom got them an apartment of their own because
Dad still won't let Starr live with him."

"Your mom?" I shook my head. I needed to quit drinking. "I
thought your mother was dead."

"Sorry. I meant Helen Dunnally, my stepmom. She's the only
mom I've ever known."

So, he must be talking about old "Hell on Wheels"—who Mom talked about when she got drunk, the one who seduced Dad and had his baby.

"You're Starr's brother?"

"That's right."

"Why is your last name Dunnally and Starr's Williams?"

"When our mom got divorced from Jerry Dunnally, she reverted to her maiden name. Starr took that name."

Over the next several hours, Sam confirmed a lot of things I already knew. Starr's mom had been a nymphomaniac and an alcoholic. The second time she cheated on Jerry Dunnally, he'd thrown her out, forever. He'd kept two-year-old Sam, who he loved. Jerry had married Helen, who was pregnant with my dad's other daughter, Amy.

I reached the absolute low point of my life in the summer of 1987. I was filled with self-loathing. I wanted to punish myself, and this is how I did it.

I went to my hated enemy. I bowed before her, and I asked her to let me be her slave. I told Cathy I would teach her everything there was to know about sapphic sex if she would acknowledge me as her "friend" when our senior year commenced. She might tell her confidants that, in my case, "friend" meant "slave." I didn't care about that. As long as I could hang with her and her crowd, I would do anything she wanted me to do.

She bought me a leather collar to seal the deal. It has a metal ring on it where a leash can be attached. I wore it every minute of every day during the summer of 1987.

Cathy Anderson's bedroom door opens to the pool area through beautifully etched glass doors. I opened those doors at midnight on the Fourth of July 1987. Fireworks lit up the western skyline. Their distant explosions could be heard faintly in Cathy's yard. As prearranged, I stood there naked, waiting for Cathy to invite me in.

"Come," she commanded.

She sat in a chair in front of her vanity mirror. She was wearing a very sexy negligee. The hose hooked to the garter belt. There were no panties. Her pubic hair had been shaved except for a small patch in the shape of a heart. The point at the bottom of the heart pointed to her vulva. She held a hairbrush in her hand. At her command, I entered the room and knelt at her feet.

"Brush my hair."

I lovingly ran the brush through her beautiful hair. I looked at her image in the mirror before us. The bra part of her negligee only supported her breasts; it did not conceal. Her nipples were erect and had been lightly rouged. I hoped at some point she would allow me to suckle her magnificent teats. I thought of the day I had first seen her, running like an Amazon goddess, with her long, blond hair flying behind her. And now, I held that hair in my hands. My dream had come true. I was overcome with emotion. Unfortunately, that caused me to yank at a snarl a bit too hard.

"Ow!" Cathy grabbed my arm and pulled me in front of her. "You stupid peasant, you've hurt me! You must be punished!" She grabbed the hairbrush out of my hand and threw me down across her knees. She spanked me with the hairbrush. She spanked me hard. I kissed her leg gratefully.

⌁

Denver, Colorado, that same night

"Stop it."

"You don't like it?"

"It's weird. It's incestuous. The guy you call dad every day is my biological father."

"It's not incestuous, Starr. Jerry's not my father, and my mom is not your mother. But never mind, I'm not in the mood anymore."

Amy took her hand out of Starr's underpants. She tried to get Starr to smell her fingers, but Starr pushed her away.

"Your mom let me move in with you, rent-free, because she thinks of us as sisters. She would be horrified if she knew you were feeling me up. That wasn't what I had in mind when I said you could come into my room. I thought you were going to tell me some news about Alys, not try to seduce me."

Not that Amy had had to try much. Starr had pretty much stayed drunk since she got to Denver. She was lying on her bed in her bra and panties when Amy knocked on her door and asked her if she was interested in some news about her "girlfriend." She'd invited Amy to join her on the bed to watch *Wheel of Fortune*. Amy had laid a hand gently on Starr's crotch and, at first, Starr had not objected. When Amy began to rub softly, Starr had closed her eyes and lain back. When Amy snuck a couple of fingers inside the panties and began to probe, Starr sighed.

But when Amy had whispered in her ear, "I'd like to buy a vowel," Starr had stopped her. It was too much like Alys. The fact that the two of them looked so much alike was eerie enough, but it was exactly the kind of joke Alys would crack at such an intimate moment.

"So, tell me," Starr asked. "What do you know about Alys?"

109

"Do you know where I was when you first got here in Denver?"

"Your mom said you had run away. She said it wasn't the first time. That was last May. I didn't see you until last week. So, where were you the past five or six weeks?"

Amy laughed. She went over to the phone and picked it up. She put a handkerchief over the receiver and said, "Alys is at Cathy's party. She's sick. She's crying and asking for you."

"It was *you*. You made that phone call."

"I also gave Candi fifty dollars to fake an interest in Alys's Dolly Partons. I gave Sarah Marsh ten dollars to tell you they were down there under the bleachers. But I think she would have done it for free just to see your face. She and I were dying with laughter."

"You cunt, why would you do that?"

"Starr, I have nothing against you. I've always liked you. But that bitch, Alys, stole my real father. He told my mom it wasn't his wife he was going back for but for the sake of his daughter. *She's* why he left us and went back to New York. I hate her and will do anything to make her life miserable. You were making her happy, Starr. I had to break you up!"

"Amy, you're crazy."

⌒⋎⋎⌒

At first it was difficult to get Cathy to play the dominant role. The sex was all new to her, and she kept wanting to know if it was all right to do this or that.

"There are some things that are out of bounds," I told her, "although I doubt they would ever occur to you. At any rate, that's what *safe words* are for. For the most part, simply think of yourself as a queen. Whatever you want, *demand.*"

That was all it took. In no time, she was the ultimate dominatrix. She insisted I refer to her as "Your Majesty."

The disappointing and somewhat hurtful thing to me was that, when she screamed a triumphant orgasm, she always called me, "Starr!"

⁓⁂⁓

Virgil worked at a lumber yard during the summer vacation and had managed to buy a '79 Mustang convertible. He was proud of it and often gave Cathy rides home from cheerleading class. He knew that Alys had moved into the pool house in Cathy's backyard. He had been swimming at Cathy's house before, and he knew there was a locked-up bomb shelter at the back of the property that was off limits to kids. Kids in bathing suits would sneak behind that huge mound of dirt and make out. The Stovall house, next door, was well lit.

"I guess they're having a party," he told Cathy. "I must have lost my invitation."

Ignoring his feeble attempt at humor, Cathy said, "My parents are there. I'm going to be there, tomorrow," she said.

"What? Why?"

"My father has arranged for us to have brunch with the Scovalls."

"Whatever for?"

"Mr. Scovall is good friends with the new head of the CIA. My dad is hoping Mr. Scovall will use his clout to get me an eventual job at the CIA."

"Are you kidding? You want to be a spy for 'the Man'? Why would you want to do that?"

Cathy sat back in her seat and looked out the window. She took a long time to answer. "Journalism tries to discover what happened in the past," she finally said. "There are analysts at the CIA, right this minute, who are discovering what *is* happening in the present.

"For example, there's an up-and-coming real estate developer named Donald Trump being feted in Moscow. They are throwing lavish parties for him, giving him the best rooms, free accommodations, and so on. They want his business, so what's the harm? Well, those rooms are bugged by the KGB. What if they catch him in a compromising position? What if he becomes wealthy enough to influence political figures in the United States? Shouldn't we know this ahead of time, instead of waiting for the journalists to catch up?"

"To what end, Cathy? To protect the plutocrats? To maintain the status quo?"

"To protect freedom, democracy, Christianity."

"Cathy, are you seriously unaware the early Christian church was communalistic? Have you never heard the words of Jesus saying, 'It's easier for a camel to get through the eye of a needle than for a rich man to get into heaven?'"

"Virgil, I don't know what happened between you and Alys. But lately you seem anti-everything."

⟨⟨⟨∿∿⟩⟩⟩

I did things that summer I had never dreamed I'd do. I thought I had chosen wisely. Teenage girls who have issues with self-loathing choose diverse ways to self-destruct. The most popular method is abuse of alcohol and drugs. Who doesn't love making yourself sick and leaving yourself defenseless around a bunch of horny guys? Some girls cut themselves. Some try to eat their problems away. It doesn't matter what method you choose. Once you passed through the limbo of "true love," all roads—lust, gluttony, greed, wrath, heresy, violence, or fraud led to hell. Only when you hit the ice of the frozen lake at the very bottom of hell, can you bounce back on your journey to Paradise.

I thought I had made myself a soft landing by choosing lust. I mean, lust is my thing! I thought Cathy and I would play BDSM games until I was over Starr, and she was over her fling with homosexuality. Even as I licked her clitoris, I thought she was bisexual. It was only when she had her hooks completely in me that I discovered that she was 100 percent mean girl.

Her mean girl Spidey senses detected my ever-growing desire for popularity. She exploited that desire with tantalizing visions of me as her number one sidekick in the coming school year. I would be her vice president on the student council. I would be her runner-up in the homecoming ceremonies. I would be the princess to her prom queen. She destroyed my will with her hissed promises.

By the time summer was over, I was hers, body and soul.

A week before school was to restart, I squatted in the corner of her room, naked, my knees spread wide as instructed. I waited with my eyes closed. I had no idea what humiliation my master had planned for me tonight. I just knew that, whatever it was, I would endure it and thank her for it afterward.

I heard the bedroom door open and close. I heard my master approach. "Are you my slave?" she asked me.

"Yes, master."

"Is your cunt my plaything?"

"Yes, master."

"Will you always obey me?"

"Yes, master."

"Open your eyes!"

Staring me in the face was Anthony Snowden's cock.

"Suck it, my little whore."

For an unforgivable split second, I considered it. Then I punched that dick right in its little eye. My knees were all pins and needles from squatting for so long, so the kick I gave him in the balls didn't have the oomph I had hoped for. Nevertheless, he felt it. He went down.

Cathy went down, backing up in fear. I looked down at that perfect body in the skimpy negligee and said, "There was only one thing that could have freed me from the spell you had me under … And you did it. Thank you."

$$\sim \mathcal{M} \sim$$

The first day of school, I was in jail. I had been arrested for vagrancy. Burk Burnett Park is comfortable in August, but the Ft. Worth police don't like you sleeping there. I first called Martha to throw my bail, but she would not accept the collect call. I guess she was still mad about the way I treated Starr. I finally had to break down and call my mom. You know what they say about family. They're the ones who, when they get a collect call from prison, have to accept the charges. Mom came and bailed me out. acting all upbeat and optimistic.

"Cheer up," she advised, "your GPA is 4.0. You are rated in the top five in Women's High School Tennis. If you can just get your head on straight, your future is bright."

I did not agree with her about my future. Cathy had betrayed me. I had never expected her to "come out" and for us to run for student body president as a gay couple. I *did* expect her to be loyal to me as a friend and make me her VP. When she shoved Anthony's cock in my face, I knew she had gone over to the dark side. I had no doubt that she would do an "Anita Bryant" on me and run on how much she hates those dirty homos.

I was one dirty homo by then. I hadn't slept in a bed in over a week. The night I had hit rock bottom at Cathy's, I had stolen her parents' best rum and hidden out in the guest house by the pool. I drank rum and listened to Lynyrd Skynyrd all night. I found some hedge shears in a tool shed and tried to cut my hair like Starr's. About 4:00 a.m., Cathy's mom came to the door and told me, "I don't know what happened between you girls, but Cathy wants you off the premises. If you don't leave, I'll have to call the police. I'm real sorry, hon."

"Really."

"Yes, I mean it."

The second day of school, I showed up with hacked-off hair; a miniskirt; and knee-high, lace-up boots. I had written "Dyke" in marker across my bloody T-shirt. I didn't even make it halfway to homeroom before Mrs. Pinkersly said, "Unuh," and led me to the Office. Just before we got there, I looked up and saw the sweetheart of Handley High walking down the stairs arm in arm with Anthony Snowden. They were making goo-goo eyes at each other. When she saw me, she was temporarily nonplussed. My bizarre appearance froze her for a second.

I took the opportunity to say as loudly as I could, "Thank you, love, for a wonderful summer!"

CHAPTER 11

THE BIG REVEAL

The summer wasn't a complete waste. When I wasn't kissing Cathy's ass, I was working on my novel. I finished it right before Labor Day and sent it to Dad.

I am legally required to attend school for another 250 days, or so. That's why I was sitting in the school cafeteria eating the gray goop when Martha and her newest boyfriend approached me. (The goop's either mashed potatoes or tapioca pudding. It's pretty good.)

Martha and Max sit at the table across from me. It's a big, long table that seats sixteen, but we're all alone. I'm required to attend school, but I don't have to bathe.

"Hi, Alys, how are you getting along?" Martha's voice is full of sympathy and hearty cheer, like a nurse talking to a dying patient.

"Sod off." (It's an English expression which means, "I'm lovely. Thanks for asking.")

"Say," Martha continued brightly, "did you hear the news? Claire Underwood is running against Cathy Anderson for class president."

Max was making a face. "Do you have a dead skunk in your pocket?" he asked me.

"Bugger off," I told him. (See above.)

"They say," Martha went on, "that nobody else is willing to oppose them. Everybody seems afraid of them."

Martha seemed to be waiting for a reply, so I said, "Fuck 'em." It occurred to me that I might be able to get through this whole conversation with two-word sentences.

"Yeah, I know you're not afraid of them. It's just that everybody else seems to think that the two of them have all the votes sewed up. You know, Cathy has all the rich, popular kids, and Claire has all the 'pole-up-their-asses' religious votes."

I didn't even need two words. "No."

"I haven't even suggested anything, yet."

"Not happening."

Martha reached across the table and took one of my hands in hers. "Wrap your writer's imagination around this: Cathy is the Sheriff of Nottingham. She demands more taxes from your poor parents. They beg for mercy. She laughs diabolically and grabs your baby brother. 'If you can't pay your taxes, I'll just take this little fellow in payment.'

"She hands the lad over to Claire. 'Here,' she says, 'take him to your priests. I'm sure they will have a lot of fun with him.' What are you going to do, Alys? Are you going to let the priests abuse your little brother?"

"For fuck's sake, Martha!" Then, realizing I'd gone over my self-imposed limit on words, I opened the floodgates. "It's futile and useless. There's no way I could ever get even 1 percent of the votes in this school. Are you forgetting, I'm a socialist, an agnostic, and a *queer*!"

"*So what?*" Martha yelled.

Martha had stood up so abruptly she'd kicked over her chair and sent it sliding three or four feet across the floor. I'd never seen her lose her cool before. She was amazing. Her face was red as the blood of her Aztec ancestors that ran through her body. Her jaw seemed set in granite. Her bosom heaved. (I had never really noticed Martha's breasts before. She actually had a pretty impressive rack.)

"What do percentages or odds or chances mean to heroes, Loxley? Do you think Don Quixote weighed the odds when he charged those windmills? Hell, no! He tilted his fool heart out. Do you think Davy Crockett considered his chances when he stepped across the line drawn in the sand? Do you imagine Audrey Murphy worried about his own ass as he wiped out half the Japanese army?

"And what about you and me, Alys? We met because you hate bullies so much. You and I have been fighting for justice since that day. Did we get rid of all the bullies in Handley High School? No! Can you win this election? *Hell, no!* But does that mean we shouldn't fight?"

Martha was on top of the table now. She spoke to the crowd of kids that gathered around us. "Should we just sit back and let the bullies walk all over us? What do you say? Who wants Alys to fight for us?"

The crowd went wild. They were yelling, and cheering, and jumping (and some of the pretty girls blew me kisses).

I pulled an imaginary sword out of an imaginary scabbard. I raised it into the air and cried, *"Off with their heads"*

Mr. Johnson gave us ten demerits each.

⌘

The motto of Cathy's campaign was "Make Handley Great Again." She handed out free caps that said "MHGA" on them. She promised to bring back all the things that had made Handley great in the past—good manners, good hygiene, and good fashion sense.

Her advisors dissuaded her from speaking on her positions on "the divine right of kings" and "judicious use of the guillotine to improve our school."

Claire's official campaign slogan was, "Vote for me, and I will mandate that the Lord's Prayer is read over the loudspeaker every morning before classes." Her unofficial smear campaign was dirtier than a bucket of fish bait. Her supporters went around the halls whispering, "Where did Cathy Anderson spend last summer? Who was she with?"

My campaign manager was Martha. She wanted me to get cleaned up, wear some nice clothes, stop cursing, and try to be nice.

We compromised. I bathed once a week.

When the tall redhead with the long, skinny legs asked me for an interview for the school paper, I didn't know she was a friend of Claire's. When she casually mentioned Anthony Snowden, I jumped right in.

"What's he even doing here?" I asked. "He's a known associate of two men who beat and raped Bianca Delgado. Why is he allowed to walk the hallways of this school a free man?"

"Are you accusing Anthony Snowden of something, Ms. Loxley?"

"The only people who can testify to Snowden's involvement in that crime have disappeared. One of them may be in 'witness protection' but neither of them are around to testify to his guilt—as you very well know, Miss ...?"

"Frazier. Julie Frazier."

"As you know ... May I call you Julie?" "Sure."

"Julie, I can't say that Anthony hired those guys to beat and rape an innocent ... well, a young girl because, in this country, we have laws that protect the rich and privileged. They get away with all kinds of shit, because our entire form of government is based on protecting the rich and entitled.

Quietly, politely, as smoothly as shit out of a goose, Julie Frazier asked me, "And how do you respond to the inevitable charges of class warfare?"

I stepped right into it. "Class warfare? Are you shitting me? The wealthy class *invented* class warfare! They stand with their foot on the workers neck, and if you dare to say, 'Could you please stop choking the lifeblood out of me?' they start screaming, 'Class warfare! Class warfare! Help! The peasants are revolting! Run for the hills!'

"I mean, how stupid can people be? It's not the Communists Americans have to fear; it's the Fascists in our own government!"

Julie was grinning like the Cheshire cat. Martha was dumping "Vote for Alys" signs in the trash can. I had pretty much ended my campaign before it began. I don't know if it was the excesses of the French Revolution or the ruthlessness of Stalin, but all you need do in this country to ruin a popular grassroots movement is identify it with Communism. On top of that, I had implied that people who feared the domino effect of Communism were stupid. About 90 percent of the American people fear the domino effect of Communism.

We went ahead and had the stupid election even though the result was never in doubt. When it was my turn to talk to my peers I said, "Hello, I'm Alys Loxley. Economically, I represent 99 percent of you. The beautiful Cathy Anderson represents the other 1 percent economically. There's another candidate, but she just represents the kooks that claim to love a man they nailed to a cross two thousand years ago. They are just a cultlike splinter group of the 1 percent.

"If the office of student body president could actually improve your life in any way, most of you would logically vote for me. But we all know that the president of the student body can do nothing. I would love to tell you that, if you voted for me, I would have beer in the soda machines, but you all know that's not true. The election of student body president is nothing more than a popularity contest. So, why do the schools not only allow it, but *insist* on it?

"It's to teach us how government works, right? To teach us about nominating candidates, voting, campaigning, the nuts and bolts of democracy, right?

"Well, I think this election has done a very good job of doing just that. Look up on the stage there. Look at that beautiful, composed, relaxed, perfect woman. Not Claire. For all her chic hairdo and expensive clothes, she's all hat and no cattle. She doesn't try to persuade the voter to support her views. She tells them, 'My way or an eternity in hell!' She'll get the coward vote, and that's all. No, I mean the lovely Cathy Anderson, the personification of years of breeding. Class, ladies and gentlemen. Cathy represents the ruling class!

"Meet the new boss, same as the *old* boss." I dragged an electric guitar out from behind a curtain and made it wail.

(This would be an excellent time to listen to the Who playing "Won't Get Fooled Again.")

The rotten fruit began to fly.

"The wealthy," I continued, "have a theory called the 'trickle-down theory.' The theory is that everything that dribbles out of the overstuffed mouths of the wealthy and trickles down off their fat laps and onto the floor is the property of the working class. The poor are allowed to fight over the scraps while the wealthy are in the vomitorium preparing for the next course."

A tomato hit me square in the forehead and splattered across my face.

"And, yes, you toadies and wannabes, you are of *our* class, not theirs. Your dads used car lot notwithstanding, they look down their noses at you."

A battery and something that looked like a saltshaker flew past my vision. Martha was heroically trying to drag me to safety.

"Well, guess what, you fucking Nazis? I'm everything the 1 percent hate: I'm a socialist. I'm an agnostic. And *I am queer!*"

I stood up straight when I yelled this and held my fist up to the sky. It's a good thing I did. My outstretched arm broke the impetus of the chair before it hit my head.

I was sitting backstage when I heard Anthony Snowden saying, "Yeah, go ahead and vote for the little queer ... *if you want a murderer for your president!*"

When I was fourteen, Mom was making me take tennis lessons from a pro at the country club. Our chauffeur would pick me up at school and drive me to the Birchwood Country Club. One day

I was running late and decided to change from my school uniform to my tennis whites in the limo. I have no control over the partition between the front seat and the back. I had no idea that Carl, the chauffeur, was watching me change.

There was a squeal of tires, a crash, and a sudden stop. I was thrown against the front seat and then bounced back into the back seat. I was stunned and just lay there for a minute. The back door opened, and Carl stuck his head in. I looked at the bra in my hand and realized I was wearing only panties. My bountiful boobs were bouncing bellicosely.

Carl stared.

A bit longer than I was really comfortable with, actually. "I'm sorry, Miss. A car ran a red light …"

Later, I thought about the way he had stared at me. It was creepy.

After my tennis lessons were done, I had to walk to the front of the country club to get to the car. One of the boys who work on the landscaping stepped in front of me. "Hey, cutie. You're all sweaty. You look like you could use a soft drink. How about letting me buy you one out of the vending machine?"

I'd had a long day. I was tired. The idea of having a drink with *any* boy, much less this knuckle dragger, was ridiculous. Plus, let's face it, I'm just a naturally rude person. So, I said, "Fuck off," and tried to walk on by.

He grabbed my arm and got right in my face. "Listen, bitch. Don't play all high and mighty with me. If I were rich, you'd be all over this cock. Let's go in these bushes over here, and I'll let you suck it."

I was terrified. I tried to pull away from him. What I should have done was *push towards him* and throw him off balance—and then kick him in the balls. My strength wasn't equal to his, and I feared I was going to be raped.

Then a man on a riding mower came into view. "What are you doing, Frank?"

I broke away then. My purse fell to the ground, and the contents went flying everywhere. I ran for the car.

<hr />

"I hold in my hand," the bastard Snowden said, "a copy of the *Handley Herald* that will be coming out tomorrow. There is a story in it concerning our own dear Alys Loxley. It seems that, when she was fourteen, she killed a boy named Frank Stone. Wow! It says here that he tried to run away, but she caught him and shot him six times!"

Even as I took the ten steps it took to get to Anthony, I could see Martha confronting Cathy. Cathy looked bewildered. She looked as surprised as we were. Max had gone in search of Stanley Scovall.

I walked up to Anthony, midspeech, and asked him, "Where did you get that?"

"Don't worry, folks. She's not armed."

"Where did you get that? Is that my juvenile record? It's supposed to be sealed. It's illegal for you to have that."

"Illegal? What about shooting some poor schlub six times?"

I tried to grab the papers out of his hands. I saw the words, "police report." Suddenly a memory was unearthed. I had kept it buried all this time.

The first shot was fired with equal parts fear and anger. He was already turning to run, and the bullet entered his inner thigh. It hit an artery, and blood began to pump out.

(For what it's worth, he would have bled out before help arrived, no matter what I had done then.) He tried to take a step, and I shot him again. He fell and tried to crawl away from me. "Please," he begged. "Please."

I felt nothing but hatred. I shot him in the head to shut him up. Then, I emptied the gun into his dick.

"It appears this bully is trying to prevent me from exercising my First Amendment right to free speech," Anthony said with an ugly sneer on his face.

He was lucky I didn't have a gun in my hand.

The lovely redheaded girl who'd trapped me into class warfare grabbed my arm and dragged me away from Anthony.

"I wrote that story for the *Handley Herald*. We need to talk." Julie led me out to the hallway.

"The envelope with the police report concerning the stabbing of Frank Stone was left on my desk sometime over the weekend. I found it when I went to class Monday. I asked Mrs. Davenport if I could use information obtained in such a way. She assured me that there was a school of thought that, since you were the only one who could legally have possession of the material, we could assume it came from you—which made it all right to publish."

"Yeah? Well, there's another school of thought," I replied, "It involves the US Constitution and the laws of the State of Texas. But I shouldn't expect the staff of the *Handley Horseshit* to know anything about that. Where is the original police report?"

"The 'original' is in possession of the Long Island Police. The copy I received is on my desk."

Julie took me to the journalism room and showed me the report. At the bottom was the signature of the police officer who had worked the case—Jane Hamilton. I immediately remembered the attractive forty-year-old who had saved my life that night.

Officer Jane Hamilton had held me in her arms in the back of an ambulance and convinced me to live that night. I had wanted to die. I didn't see how I could go on living. "Followers of Lilith are survivors," she told me. "I know you saw her. Don't be afraid. You are not alone."

I had blanked that conversation out of my memory as well. Now, I remembered the relief I felt. Maybe I wasn't crazy, after all.

"Where's the envelope it came in?" I asked Julie.

"I don't know. It was thrown away."

"Do you remember anything about it?"

"No."

"Think!"

"The return address! That's right. It said Stanley something on it."

"Are you sure?"

"Yes."

"Excellent," I pulled the attractive redhead close to me. I said, sotto voce, "It seems like a cover-up to me. What do you think?"

"Well, Ms. Loxley, I—"

"Please. Mrs. Loxley is my mom. Call me Alys. By the way, do your friends call you Red?"

"No, I'm just Julie."

"Well, just Julie, I have a question. Does the carpet match the drapes?"

Julie Frazier was trying to beat me to death with her purse when Martha pulled her off me. "What the hell is going on here?" she asked.

"Just a misunderstanding," I assured her.

"*She*," Julie said, pointing at me, "is not a nice person. Not a nice person at all."

CHAPTER 12

GOODBYE YELLOW-BRICK ROAD

"What is wrong with you?" Martha asked me when we were safely away from the homicidal Julie Frazier. "You can't come on to the editor of the school paper! You can't ask her the color of her pubic hair! What's wrong with you, Alys? Are you fucking crazy?"

"You know, I don't think she even fancies girls."

"Of course, she doesn't. Why is it so hard for you to accept that most women do not see you that way? Ninety percent of us only feel sexual attraction for men. Get over it!"

"She's lying, you know."

"About the color of her pubic hair or only liking guys?"

"No, no. Forget that, Watson. Tell me this: What's point of discreetly placing an object on someone's desk on a weekend when she's not there?"

"A secret admirer?"

"Jolly good, Watson! Quite admirable! You've thrown a hammer over your shoulder and hit the nail right on the head. As you've so cleverly deduced, the whole point is anonymity. So, why secrete a package and leave your name on the return address?"

"Doesn't 'secrete' mean 'to ooze out'?"

"You're a journalism major?"

"Well, I'm considering changing over to criminology."

"Please do. No, Bertie Wooster, my 'little gray cells' tell me she's lying to divert the attention of the world's greatest detective (as well as the world's best lesbian lover) from the real culprit."

"Are you doing Sherlock Holmes or Poirot right now?"

"I was thinking Inspector Jacques Clouseau."

"Your French accent sucks. So, Julie is lying about Stanley being the source. So, who was it?"

"Search me." But even as I said it, I thought back to my last conversation with Virgil Wilder.

"Try to get your head around it, Martha. I'm a murderer."

"But the police report says you were being raped at the time. That makes it self-defense."

And that's the $64,000 question. Was Saint Agnes right when she told me to leave justice to the great male God in the sky? Or was

Lilith right when she chided me for my cowardice and said, "He has it coming"?

And, just like that, my shot at high school popularity was over. Not only was I *not* popular; I was shunned. I was a pariah. People looked at me and saw a girl who had shot somebody to death.

Cathy won the election, of course. It irked me a bit how easily she won. She never broke a sweat. She just sat there, being her beautiful self and waving at her adoring supporters with that annoying Queen Elizabeth II wave. Everything had always come easily for Cathy—all her life.

I decided to visit my half sister, Amy Dunnally, over spring break. I called ahead, but I was unable to reach Amy. I talked to her mother, Helen Dunnally (nee Wheeler). I asked her if Amy would be home over break.

"Both the girls are staying home during break," she assured me. "I talked to them just recently, and they both said they had no plans to do anything special over the break."

"She has a roommate?"

"Yes, her cousin, Starr, is staying with her. I've rented them the cutest little apartment just across the river."

"Do you think they would mind if I stayed with them for a few days?"

"Oh, I'm sure Amy is dying to meet you. Starr has been telling her so much about you."

No doubt. This should be interesting.

———⁓———

It was 45 and sunny the day I arrived in Denver. I had borrowed Mom's car because my old Honda Civic would not have made it on the eight hundred-mile journey. The instructions I had been given were good, and I arrived at Amy and Starr's place on time.

Starr wasn't there. Amy didn't seem to want to talk about her. "She's gone to Quantico," was all she would say.

I had expected Amy to look a little like me because we have the same dad, so that didn't surprise me. What did surprise me was that Amy was noticeably pregnant.

"It's Stanley's baby," she told me when she saw me looking at her distended belly. "Hopefully, we'll be married before it arrives."

In my world view, it was kinda miraculous that Stanley and Amy could be having a baby, because, until this very moment, I had Stanley pegged as a Ft. Worth boy and Amy as a distant, possibly imaginary figure of folklore. I was slowly putting it together that there had to be some traveling and intermingling of the two, but before I could follow up on that line of thought, Amy went into full attack mode.

"You're prettier than me. That figures."

How do you answer something like that?

"When was the last time you saw Father?"

The idea of Dad being this obnoxious girl's father was so bizarre I just sort of sat there, gaping.

"Tall white guy, dark hair, green eyes. That jog your memory?"

"Um, let's see. I last saw Dad when he entered the courtroom for his sentencing. We all knew he was going away for a long time. I was crying. I ran up to him and I said, 'Dad, people are saying that you're a thief. It's not true, is it?'

"Dad picked me up and swung me around in a complete circle and said, "Yar, darlin', you know very well, *I'm a pirate!*' Then he kissed me and went into court.

"I so fucking hate you!" Amy screamed at me. "*Do you know what I would do for one little hug from that man?*"

I swear if Amy had a gun, I'd be dead right now. (You hear that, NRA?)

"And you, you little, ungrateful, spoiled brat; when was the last time you visited him?"

"I haven't been able—"

"Do you even know where the facility is where he's being held?"

"I think it's somewhere in North Carolina."

"Butner, twenty-five miles northeast of Raleigh. Guess who's not on the visitor's list?"

"You know, Amy, I don't think we can help him much by visiting. The last time I talked to him, his biggest gripe was that he had to make a reservation three days in advance to get a tennis court."

I thought this was pretty funny. Amy didn't think so.

Then something really embarrassing happened. This hadn't happened before. Lilith had had only spoken *to* me, never through me. I began talking, and it was my voice and everything, but the words … weren't mine! "Somewhere, in some universe, our fates are reversed."

Talk about a conversation stopper. But Amy managed to come up with a rejoinder.

"Our fates were almost reversed right here in this universe. Our father was going to come live with my mother and me, but a third member of their criminal enterprise lied to Mom and told her that Scott had sold out his partners for immunity. Scott was in custody at the time and couldn't defend himself from her slander. With me on the way, Mom couldn't stick around to see who was telling the truth. She came back to Denver and hooked up with her previous lover, Jerry Dunnally. If Jill hadn't got through with her lying phone call, you would have been the one without a dad."

"Makes you think," I said.

"Speaking of thinking," I said, looking at Amy, "what were you thinking giving my arrest report to Julie Frazier?"

"I don't know any Julie Frazier. I gave the report to Virgil Wilder the last time I was in Fort Worth to see Stanley. I thought he should know the kind of woman he had fallen in love with."

I thought about how thin the line was between love and hate. Virgil had remembered what I said about killing a man and told Julie. I am definitely not good with men. "How did you get it?

"I intercepted all the letters you wrote to Starr last summer. In one of them you mentioned a Jane Hamilton from Long Island. I went to visit her."

"And played the 'long-lost little sister, right?"

"Worse."

"Oh, my god. You didn't."

"Yeah. I seduced the old broad and blackmailed her for the report."

My half sister has depths of depravity I had not imagined. "You're sick, Amy.

"Would you tell Starr I came by?" I asked as I was leaving, "Tell her I'd like to see her at the prom if she can forgive me." I didn't really expect anything to come of it.

CHAPTER 13

THE INEVITABLE PROM NIGHT MURDER

Suzie Kwan, my doubles partner, asked me to the prom, which was pretty nice (and pretty brave) considering I was so despised at Handley. I refused. I didn't want her to suffer from my "untouchable" status.

"Find a nice boy and go with him," I suggested, "maybe even have sex with him. I want you to have the happy conventional memories of prom night."

"Just because I've never killed a guy doesn't mean I'm bi, Alys."

So, now Suzie's mad at me too. Where's that can of worms when you need it?

In the novel I wrote, Henry VIII is condemned to spend the rest of his life in a cell in a dungeon. The walls of the dungeon are covered with portraits of all his victims. Prominently on display were the two wives he had executed—Anne Boleyn, and poor little Cat Howard.

I was punishing myself in the same manner. I was languishing on my lonely bed reading a book called *Wyrd Sisters* by Terry Pratchett. Every time I raised my head from the book, I found myself looking at a framed picture of Starr.

Ever since Cathy hooked up with Anthony Snowden, I have noticed occasional bruises on her arms and neck. I didn't pay any attention. If they enjoyed rough sex, that was their business. I was not going to interfere. I felt I owed her nothing.

About ten o'clock the phone rang. It was Martha. "Alys, get down to the hospital as quick as you can. It's Cathy. It looks bad."

"She's been raped and beaten," Martha told me upon my arrival. "Max is on the phone with the police, but it's unclear what happened."

The emergency room was full of kids who had come straight from prom. Many were still in their fancy dress, and the scene resembled a Fellini film.

"You know the little brunette girl, Sarah?" Stanley asked me. "She went out for a smoke at the Prom and found her." He leaned in close to me and whispered, "She also saw Anthony Snowden driving away."

I escaped the horrible nightmare that was that emergency room by imagining it was the previous summer with Cathy. She could be cruel. Once she led me into her bedroom on a leash. I was on my hands and knees. The two highest-ranking mean minions were sitting on her bed. They laughed as she forced me to eat out of a bowl on the floor. (It was well-done hamburger meat.)

That may sound horrible to straights. But the thing is, I'm a submissive, and if she had ordered me to perform cunnilingus on her, I would have willingly (and gladly) done it.

Stanley left. People came and went. I rehearsed what I was going to tell her when it was all over, and she was all right. "Stop pretending to be straight. It's not worth it. You're too good and too wonderful to have to deal with boys."

Someone sat down next to me. He laid a magazine on the armrest between us. "There's something that might help on page 5," he said and rose to leave. I looked up at him. It was Joe Scarvino.

"We're even now," he mouthed and then walked away.

I opened the magazine to page 5. Someone had scrawled:

Arlington Motel

1206 W. Division

Arlington, TX

Room 224

I tore the page out and put it in my pocket. I found Martha and said, "I need transport."

Max handed over the keys to his truck without comment. I clutched the paper in my pocket. It was common knowledge that, when people like Anthony Snowden wanted drugs, they got them from somebody like Joe Scarvino. Such transactions took place in lowdown dives like the Arlington Motel.

By now, the waiting room was nearly deserted. Most of those remaining were asleep. A nurse came into the waiting room. She looked upset.

"Is everything all right?" I asked.

"The patient has gone into a coma. She might survive. But with the brain damage, well …"

She wouldn't say it, but the message I was receiving was that it might be better if she didn't.

I got in Max's truck and drove to the motel. On the way, I said out loud, "What do you think, Lilith?"

Nothing. Silence.

"Well? Should I kill this guy or not?"

Obviously, Lilith was covering her ass. Whatever happened, she couldn't be blamed for it.

By the time I got to the motel, I had still not received divine guidance. As usual, I was going to have to decide my fate myself. I climbed the stairs and walked down to room 224. I heard a female voice crying. I didn't hesitate. I kicked in the door.

Anthony Snowden's body lay on the floor, his head surrounded in a pool of blood. Starr sat in a chair, her head in her hands saying, "It's my fault. It's all my fault."

Despite the shock, I should have noticed important details. I should have registered the lack of blood on Starr's clothing. I should have noticed that there was no murder weapon anywhere in the room. My concern, though, was with Starr. I had not seen her in nearly a year. Seeing her again made my heart burst with love. She was distraught. Tears streamed down her face. My only thought was to remove her from this horrid situation.

I grabbed her arms and helped her out of the chair.

"Where's your car?" I asked her.

With me supporting her, we were able to get down to the parking lot and find her car. I put her behind the wheel.

"Go straight back to Denver right now," I instructed.

"I need to wait for—"

"Wait for nothing, Starr. Get going. Now."

Starr drove off. I went back up to the room. First, I wiped of any surface that Starr might have touched. Then I started yelling. I threw things around the room. I knocked over lamps and broke everything I could break. When I was sure I had drawn a crowd, I lifted the body over my head and carried it out on the balcony. A dozen witnesses stood around wondering what all the noise was about.

"No means no, you son of a bitch," I yelled for the benefit of the crowd and threw the body over the rail.

Then I went home and finished my Terry Pratchett book.

CHAPTER 14

THE USUAL SUSPECT

Mom woke me up the next morning. She shook my shoulder and said, "Alys, Alys. There are policemen at the door." Mom was acting weird. She brushed her fingers gently across my cheek. "Is everything all right, hon?"

"I don't know," I answered. "Did they see Peterskin in his underwear?"

The male cop was old, thin, balding, and had an attitude. The female cop was an attractive black woman in her twenties.

"I'm Detective Lenny Briscoe," the old guy said. "This is Officer Butler. We'd like to ask you some questions."

I looked at the female cop. "Is Cathy dead?"

"Oh, no." She instinctively stretched out a reassuring hand but stopped herself. "She's still in a coma, but she's alive." I could tell she was a sympathetic, kind person. She obviously had no future in policework.

"Why don't y'all come in, and I'll make some coffee," Mom said.

Both police officers chose to remain standing.

"Where were you last night between 1:00 a.m. and 1:30 a.m.?" Detective Briscoe asked me.

"I was either in bed or getting ready for bed. You know, I'm pretty sure Cathy's nurse will remember me. She took me in to talk to Cathy. She led me out of Cathy's room at about eleven."

"And can you tell us your whereabouts for the two hours after that?" Briscoe asked. "What's this all about, Officers?"

"Did you know Anthony Snowden?"

"*Did* I?"

"Alys," the cop named Nan said sympathetically. "Antony Snowden was found dead at the Arlington Motel on Division Street this morning at 2:00 a.m."

"Someone fitting your description was seen throwing the victim off the balcony of the ArlingtonMotel on West Division last night," Briscoe informed me. You got an alibi or not?"

"Am I the only person who can't account for my every minute last night?"

"The only one who's killed somebody before," Briscoe responded.

"I want a lawyer."

Detective Briscoe nodded at Officer Butler, "Book her, Nano."

I was sitting in the back seat of a police car. Officer Nan Butler was driving. Detective Briscoe was in the passenger seat, smoking a cigarette.

"I'd like to investigate the scene of the crime, Lenny."

"What for? It's a waste of time. This is an easy one, kid. We'll book her tonight. Tomorrow we'll put her in a lineup. We got half a dozen witnesses that saw her kill the vic. Easy-breezy."

"Come on, Lenny. This is my first murder. I'd like to savor the experience."

"Tell you what. Isn't there a Bob's Big Boy close to that motel, over on University? Drop me off there and go check out the scene. Come back for me when you're done."

"Deal."

We dropped the detective off next to the plastic statue of a fat boy in checked overalls holding a tray of burgers.

"Try the chocolate malts," I suggested. "They're delish."

"Go murder somebody," Briscoe replied.

I've heard of a thing called "gaydar" that is supposed to let you know if a girl likes you (you know, in that special way.) If there is such a thing, mine's broken. I was really attracted to Nan Butler, but I had no idea if she liked me. I decided to try and break the ice.

"Hey, Nan, what did the Buddhist monk say to the hot dog vendor?"

Nan didn't answer me, but I think she was just concentrating on the traffic.

"Make me one with everything," I said.

Nan looked at me in the mirror. "You know," I said, waving my arms expressively, "everything!"

Nan's eyes went back to the road, but she was smiling. Who knows? Maybe she likes me.

Nan was supposed to keep me locked in the police car at the motel.

"Actually," she told me, "I should have taken you downtown first and then come back, but that's a lot of driving and a waste time. You won't try to run off, will you?"

"Promise."

She put me in cuffs, and we went up to Room 224. Nan pulled out a knife and cut through the police tape. We went in. Anthony's body was gone, but there was still a big stain on the floor where his head had been.

"This where you killed him?" Nan asked.

"What? No, I didn't kill him."

"Ha! Almost tricked you there, didn't I?"

Nan is the prettiest cop I've ever seen, but she's no Kojak. "It's funny," she said. "There's almost no blood down there where he landed, but there's a lake of blood up here." She began moving about the small room, looking for clues. She found something and with a pair of tweezers, she pushed it into an evidence bag. She held it up for me to see. It was a vitamin container. It said, "Rainbow Light Prenatal One Multivitamins."

"This," Nan averred, "means something."

She led me out the door and began to replace the police tape on the door.

"That's definitely her," a girl said, pointing her long fingernails at me. "I remember looking at her as she held that big guy over her head. I thought, *Geez, for a little girl, she sure is strong*! Then she yelled, 'Hasta la Vista, baby!" and threw him over the rail. My first thought was, *Gee, she must really hate him*. My second thought was, *That was the worst Arnold Schwarzenegger imitation I've ever heard.*"

"Thank you," Officer Butler said. "We appreciate your help. You can go now."

"You're not much of a detective, are you?

"What do you mean?"

"You didn't ask me if I had seen her before. The fact is, I saw this crazy bitch escort some dyke-looking girl out of that second-story room and down the stairs to a car about half an hour earlier. The car had Colorado license plates."

CHAPTER 15

ALLIANCES

"Well, this is another fine mess you've got us into."

Lilith had apparently joined me in my cell in the Tarrant County Jail and done so in a jovial mood.

"What are you so happy about?"

"Are you kidding me, kid? Don't you read the newspapers? This story has gone nationwide! 'Teenage Girl Avenges Best Friend's Rape—Hurls Assailant off Second-Story Balcony!' It's great Press. When the reporters start coming around begging for an interview, remember what to tell them."

"Lilith made me do it?"

"Not like that. You tell them, 'He had it coming. He deserved to die and the demigoddess, Lilith, chose me to mete out justice. Women will no longer wait for the patriarchy to punish their own.'"

"You know I didn't actually kill the guy, don't you?"

"Shh! Keep that to yourself. I need a celebrity to get my name out there. 'Infamous' is as good as 'famous.' There is no such thing as bad publicity. The only bad thing is anonymity. An obscure high school girl is *not* going to get my name out there. Just go with it."

"But I'm beginning to have my doubts that Starr did it. She said, 'It's my fault,' not, 'I killed him.'"

"Don't puss out on me now, kid. You're about to have your fifteen minutes of fame."

"Yeah, and when my fifteen minutes is up, the state of Texas is going to give me a lethal injection."

"Kid, wake up and smell eternity. If my existence shows you nothing else, it must open your eyes to the fact that death is just a transition into your next life. I don't know why mortals can't see it. It's all around them. Life is a cycle of birth, death, and rebirth. Every winter, death comes. And every spring, rebirth arrives without fail.

"Why would anyone want to live past a hundred years? Would you want to keep driving your '69 Honda Civic the rest of your life?"

"Easy for you to say. I don't turn eighteen until next week. *I,* Alys Loxley, have a whole life ahead of me. I don't want to die before I'm twenty and come back as someone named Jill. Or worse," I said in horror, "Jack!"

"I'm disappointed, kid. I guess you're like every other scared little mortal, clinging to your miserable existence instead of bravely facing your destiny."

"Eat shit, Lilith."

My grandmother surprised me by getting me one of the best defense lawyers in the country.

Wilma Kunsler had become famous in the sixties defending student radicals during the Vietnam War. I thought Grandmother had done me a great service until I found out that she and Wilma were old friends, and Wilma had taken the case pro bono.

"The good news," she told me, "is that I've talked the judge out of denying you bail.

"The bad news," she added, "is that she's set bail at five million dollars. Make yourself comfortable. You're going to be here for a while."

There was a basketball court in the basement level of the jail on Main and Throckmorton. On the street level there were vents so straight people could hear (and even see, if they wanted to squat) the cons playing basketball. I was watching a pickup game from the bleacher. Or rather, I was watching a magnificent pair of legs running back and forth. The black skin of these perfectly shaped legs glistened with sweat. I would have given the bologna sandwich I had for lunch to be able to lick that sweat off those legs. A terrible shot boinked off the side of the backboard and bounced toward me. I retrieved it and tore my eyes off those legs and looked up into the face of …

"*Nan?*"

"I guess you must have got arrested by my sister, Nan. My name's Zana, Zana Butler."

"God, Zana, I can't believe we met like this. I mean it must be kismet or Xanadu or some shit like that. There's so much I want to know about Nan. Could you give me a few minutes?"

Zana threw the ball to other players and sat next to me. "Whatcha wanna know about Nan?"

"Does she like girls?"

"She's crazy about Janet Jackson."

"You know what I mean. I think I may be in love with her. Do you think she could love me back?"

"What did she arrest you for?"

"Murder."

"Hmm. What did you say your name was?"

"Alys."

"Alys, I'm pretty sure my sister is as gay as you are. She just hasn't admitted it yet. But gay or straight, my sister will never have anything to do with a murderer."

"Well, shit." I should have thought of that myself. Nan is a good person, and, even if I didn't kill Anthony, I was a murderer. I decided to change the subject. "Did your sister arrest you?"

"No, that was some of her brothers in the police force. They arrested me for exercising my right to free speech. We were protesting Reagan's veto of the Civil Rights Restoration Act of 1987. We're trying to get congress to override his veto."

"That's ridiculous. Demonstrating peacefully for minorities' civil rights isn't illegal."

"No, but what you want to do with my sister is, at least in Texas."

"What?"

"In 1973, Texas passed a law that made 'homosexual conduct' a criminal act. Federal laws have overridden that law, but it's still on the books in Texas. You need to wake up and realize you all are a minority, too. The white ruling class is also a patriarchy."

"Wow. Thanks for teaching me so much today. You've given me a lot to think about. I just have one more question for you. Would you find me a place for a woman's church?"

A week later, I had a visitor by the name of Eirene Worthinghampton. She was the same age as me, but she was dressed in the long, flowing robe of a Buddhist monk. She said she was the proprietress of the Worthinghampton Orphanage, which was located on the top of a hill overlooking Lake Worth. The building was an old mansion that had been renovated and repurposed as an orphanage in the 1950s.

"My daddy donated the building," she told me. "But he is loath to spend any more on maintenance and upkeep. When I returned from my training to become a monk in Bangkok, Daddy said I could run the place. I discovered that, for the last six years, the place has been kept going mainly by the evangelical preaching of a child prodigy named Chloe.

"She's been preaching at evangelical tent meetings since she was seven. She's hugely popular. She thinks she's ready to make the jump to weekly sermons from Will Rogers Auditorium."

"Down by the stock yards?"

"Right. She thinks she can fill two thousand seats a week. Plus there will be broadcasts from KJKS, 830 on your AM dial."

"Well, that's great for the little tyke. So, what's the problem?"

"The problem is that it's going to take a significant initial investment to make this happen."

"Hey, I'm broke. I think the government seized my trust fund along with all of Dad's other assets. I have no money to give her."

"She doesn't want your money, Ms. Loxley; she wants your soul."

⌒⁓⁓

I got to see Chloe "perform" that night at an outdoor "tabernacle." And what a performance it was. I could imagine how cute she must have been when she was seven doing this.

Her long, blond hair fell to her waist. Her dress was as white as an angel's robe, although it stopped two inches above her knees. She held a Bible in her hands, which seemed extra large in her small hands. She sang "The Old Rugged Cross,' and I swear there were tears flowing all over that tent.

Then she got into her message, which the crowd really loved. "Everyone in heaven owns their own planet," she said. "Of course, if you want to go visit your family or friends, you have a rocket ship at your disposal. You will have a huge mansion and servants to heed your beck and call. And these servants will be grateful for being in heaven and having the opportunity to serve you there. They won't talk back, and they won't steal.

"The faithful will gather each day for huge dinners, prepared by the staff. Those who have been particularly obedient will get to sit close to Jesus. You will be able to eat to your heart's content without getting a stomachache. There will be wine for the elders and lots of Big Red for the women and children. You will know your parents and children in heaven, and even if you died when you were thirty, and your child died when she was ninety, she'll still call you mother, and you will call her your little girl. Everyone will be happy all the time and obey the elders because, if they don't … well, they'd better pack some sunscreen because they're going someplace hot!"

The crowd roared with laughter.

"Just be sure you are saved," Chloe continued. "If you haven't taken the Lord Jesus Christ as your savior, do it now, while there is still a place in heaven for you."

After the show, Eirene took me backstage to meet Chloe.

"That was quiet a performance," I told her.

"I know you are, but what am I?"

She may be a child prodigy, but she's still a little brat.

CHAPTER 16

THE SCAM

"You know I fantasize about having visitors all the time in my lonely cell. I expected my mom to come visit me, since she's my mom and all. But in fact, she's only come round once in the last three weeks. I've thought about the folks from *Entertainment Tonight* coming by because people in here keep saying I'm all over the news. I've even, late at night when I'm touching myself, imagined that it was Starr come to see me. But I've never, in my wildest imagining, considered the idea that I might get a visit from *my arresting officer.*"

"Does it make you uncomfortable?" Nan asked. I can leave. Do you want me—"

"No, no. It's great to see you. I can't tell you how pleased I am."

"Yeah, well, that's the thing. Zana told me that you, you know, like me and stuff."

"I'm glad she did. I really wanted to get that out there so you could react (or not) anyway you wanted. I mean if you totally hated me, you could have just ignored that and walked away forever."

"Alys, you didn't kill Anthony Snowden, did you?"

"No, I didn't, Nan. But don't most people in here say that?"

"That they didn't kill Anthony Snowden?"

And then we were both laughing, and we were on the same page, and we relaxed, and we talked, and I haven't felt this good since before Starr saw me kiss Cathy.

Before she left, Nan told me she was going to be on vacation for the next two weeks. "I'm going to take a little trip to Denver. I'm going to find that car. I'm going to find the one who really killed Snowden. I'm getting you out of here."

"You may not find that car in Denver, Nan. You might find out that it's moved on to Quantico."

"Can't you just tell me?"

"Maybe in some future lifetime I may be able to outgrow the idea that there's nothing worse than a rat, but I'm not there yet. Sorry, hon."

Black girls *can* blush.

The next day, I had more visitors. Eirene sat there with her arms crossed and wouldn't even pick up the phone. Chloe pretended that the phone wasn't working, and she couldn't hear me. She kept making these exaggerated puzzled looks and mimed, *What? What did you say?* Finally, Eirene took the phone and said, "This is all her idea. I'm just here because a minor can't come in here without an adult." Then she handed the phone back to Chloe.

She said, "I'm a genius, lady. I have an IQ of two hundred. Would you believe that?"

"No."

"OK. Well, I don't even know if IQs go as high as two hundred, so I'll accept your skepticism. Anyway, here's my plan. I arrange to hold a 'prisoner revival' for all you jailbirds. You come down the aisle crying and beating your chest." (She glanced at my chest when she said that, and her eyes widened.) "So, anyway you're saying, 'Forgive me, Lord. I repent of my evil ways,' and all that; and I step up and put my hand on your shoulder and say, 'Hold your head up high, oh wretched creature; for today you have been forgiven for your sins!' What do you think?"

"What's in it for me?"

"Money, stoops! We'll make a pile. I can see the headline now: 'Child Evangelist Saves Cold-Blooded Killer's Soul'! We'll make a ton of cash. What, you don't have any need for money?"

Lilith kicked my ankle. I don't know how she did it, being incorporeal and all, but she made me feel like I'd just been kicked in the ankle.

"OK, fine," I grumbled. "Let's do this thing."

I was lying on my bunk reading a Margaret Atwood novel, when the prettiest girl you ever saw in a prison jumpsuit came up to me and said, "Could I be your bitch?"

I had seen her earlier in the day, in the gym. Partly to make Zana proud but mostly out of perversity, I had joined three black girls playing against four white girls in a game of basketball.

The white girls' strategy was simple. A giant of a girl named Eileen would stand under the basket with her arms up. The other girls would throw the ball in the general direction of the backboard, and Eileen would drop it in for a score. There was no ref to keep her out of the three- second lane or to keep her from goaltending on defense.

I caught a pass at half court and decided that we were going to score at least one goal. I ran straight for Eileen who was planted in front of the goal like a big, old oak tree. I climbed that goddamn oak tree to make a goal. I planted my right foot on her tree-limb size thigh, rose up, pushed off her shoulder with my left foot, and slam dunked it.

Eileen sat on her butt, looking dazed and confused, until her pea-sized brain registered what had happened. She caught me and put me in a chokehold. I managed to elbow her in the solar plexus and break free. The same punch that broke her nose banged her head down on the hardwood floor of the gym.

Now, the young girl who witnessed that was in my cell offering herself to me.

It made sense. When you are in the jungle, you're going to get fucked. You might as well choose a way that you might have a little control over.

I tried to sit up, but there was a huge weight on my chest. I found I was being crushed under a ton of grief. I wanted to sob, but I wouldn't do that to the little girl. I would not show any weakness. I rolled over toward the wall so she would not see me cry.

When sad little schoolgirl me got her widdle-biddy feelings hurt by Cathy, she came up with this coolly cynical perspective on life: Rutting and power are all there is."

Suddenly the floor dropped out from under me, and I realized it was true. It wasn't just a dramatic pose of a spoiled teenager. The world really was a cold, cruel place. I was filled with despair.

"I'll protect you," I managed to say. I rolled over and looked at the little waif. She had to be at least eighteen. Otherwise, she would be in juvie. She didn't look like it, though. She looked to be no more than sixteen. She looked a bit like the young girl I had been just before I'd killed Frank Stone.

"Thank you," she said, relieved. She looked around and asked, "What now? Do you want me to take my clothes off? It's kinda public here. I mean, people come and go during free period."

"What's your name?" I asked.

"Evie. Evie Whitebread."

"Do I detect a French accent?"

"Oui, my mother is French."

"Evie, come here and get in the bed with me."

She obeyed, and we lay spooning on the bunk bed. I whispered in her ear, "You're safe now. As long as I'm around, you never need to fear rape or harm of any kind."

We both lay there crying—she, from relief and I, thinking of all those girls out there with no protection.

※

I was working in the laundry when a guard came up to me and said there was a call for me. This was unheard of. Prisoners do not receive calls. Not only that but the guard took me right up to administration. There was nothing between me and the outside world but a glass door! I picked up the receiver that was lying there. "Hello?"

Unbelievably, it was my dad. I'm quite sure this was the first time in history that a prisoner had been able to put through a call to another prisoner.

"Hey, Princess. I got some great news for you! You are a hot item! Everybody is talking about the high school girl who killed the chap who raped her best friend. And get this: Random House has offered a million dollars for the publishing rights to your book."

"Dad, my book is a fantasy novel of the sixteenth century."

"It doesn't matter what your book is about. It could be a book on the manufacture of cat food. With your name on it, everyone's going to want to buy it! I'll get the paperwork to you as soon as I can. As soon as we sign, you can use the million bucks to post your bail. You will be a free woman!"

"I'm not sure I can leave right now, Dad. There's someone who needs me here."

"Don't be a sap. You can help more from the outside. Listen, there's a literary agent who remembers rejecting your query. He wants to know if you can ever forgive him?"

"Tell him to eat shit and die."

As I was escorted back to my job in the laundry, the lights flickered mysteriously in the hallway.

"Is that you?" I whispered into a freshly laundered sheet.

"Yeah, I was in Pakistan, celebrating the election of Benazir Bhutto as prime minister, when I heard the good news. Congrats, baby. Now we can get started on my church. We've wasted enough time."

"I think I'm just going to stay here until my trial."

"You what? Oh, fuck no! Look, I'm a woman. That means I can multitask. Before I zoomed over to Pakistan, I was spying on Zana Butler, and I happen to know that she's on her way here with some good news about a location for our church. Everything is looking up! I'm going to have a church telling my side of the story, and you are going to have all the nookie you've ever dreamed of."

"I don't care about that anymore."

"You what? Don't tell me you've had a religious experience! Listen, I'll tell you the same thing I tell everybody who has a religious experience—don't worry; you'll get over it!"

"It wasn't so much a religious experience as a 'reality' experience. It was more painful than the Easter Bunny or the Tooth Fairy. It was more painful than Santa Claus. It was even more painful than the realization that the wait for Jesus's return was going to be a long, long wait.

"I realized there are no gods or goddesses out there who will help us make the world better. It hurt, but I can take pain. I can take the empty feeling and the crushing sadness. You know why? Because I believe in *me*. I am still standing. I will fight the bastards, even if I have to do it all by myself."

"And what am I, chopped liver? Am I not proof that life goes on after death? Am I not proof of the spiritual and the miraculous?"

"You are probably a tumor in my brain. You are some manifestation of my mental illness. And even if you were real, so what? Life may go on after death, but so does cruelty, poverty, and disease."

"Punk. Nihilist. I can't talk to you when you're like this."

I don't know what crawled up her ass. Once she had gone, I began to feel better. I had accepted the fact that the only thing I knew for certain was that I was going to live a certain number of days, and then I would die. I didn't care. I was determined to live each of those days in a manner that would make *me* proud. Nothing else mattered. I had given up my immature dream to be the Legendary Lesbian Lothario.

CHAPTER 17

ALL THE LONELY PEOPLE

There are rooms in the county courthouse where prisoners and lawyers can have private conversations. I sat in one with my lawyer, Wilma Kunsler, and Officer Nan Butler.

"They assure me these rooms are private. No cameras, no bugs," Ms. Kunsler told me. "Officer Butler told me she wanted to talk to you about the case. I told her no way unless I was in attendance. So, I have to be here. However, Officer Butler has informed me that the gist of the conversation is of a personal nature, so ..."

Ms. Kunsler put her feet up on the desk and closed her eyes. "Feel free to make out," she said and began to pretend to snore.

We both smiled at each other. "Wanna make out?" I asked her.

"I'm looking forward to it, but maybe under different circumstances."

"I agree."

"Alys ... hon." She managed to say the word that had made her blush when I said it to her.

I reached out and held her hand in mine. Wilma's eye popped open for one second and then closed again.

"Before I drove eight hundred miles to Colorado with nothing more than a partial license plate number, I went ahead and interviewed everyone I could find who knew Anthony and Cathy. Anthony was pretty much universally hated. One student told me the story of Anthony hitting a homeless guy up on Lancaster Avenue with his car. He drove it all the way home with a homeless guy stuck in the windshield. He told his daddy's mechanic he needed a new windshield. He won't be missed.

"A little brunette girl named Sarah told me an interesting story about a girl named Starr who used to date you and found you kissing Cathy."

Wilma stopped fake snoring and said, "Don't say anything, Alys."

"Sarah said that Starr then moved to Denver, Colorado, to live with her cousin, Amy," Nan continued. "She gave me an address."

Because we held hands, Nan felt the slight, involuntary twitch of my fingers when she said that. Otherwise, I was impassive.

"Alys, if Starr ... well, if Starr cared about you at all, she wouldn't let you take the rap for something you didn't do."

"It's more complicated than that, Nan."

"My client has nothing further to say."

And that was that.

When I returned to my cell, Evie jumped up from my bed and ran to me and gave me a kiss on the cheek.

"How was your day, dear?" she asked.

"We need to talk, Evie."

"Don't tell me; you're eloping with your secretary."

"Seriously, Evie. I need to know what you're in here for. I need to know how long you're staying. I've been given an opportunity to get out of here. And I need to know if I can take you out, too, or if I can get you out first, or what."

"Alys, that's great news. You, of course, need to get out of here if you can; but is there really any way you could get me out with you?"

"I don't know. I've got one of the best defense attorneys in the country. What were you arrested for?"

"I was arrested for possession with the intent to distribute."

I hate drugs. I think Evie could see that on my face.

"I'm sorry, Alys. My boyfriend got me hooked. He made me sell the shit, too."

"Well, there's your defense."

The lights in my cell started flickering. "Oh, shit. Evie, listen. I've got a lot of things I need to think about. Could you go out in the common area for a bit?"

"Alys! What about all those mean women out there? Suppose one of them tries to—"

"OK. It's just that I have to go to the bathroom."

We both looked over at the toilet attached to the wall of my cell, in plain sight.

"I get it," Evie said. "OK, I'll take my chances with the ogres." She kissed me on the cheek and left.

"Hey kid, it's me."

"Yeah, I saw the lights blinking. Thanks for the heads up."

"No prob. I'm glad to see you're in a better mood. Listen, I just have a minute. Zana Butler just signed in at visitor registration. She's signed a lease on a place for the church. Are you ready to get out there and start spreading the good news of Lilith's return?

"I've been thinking about that, Lilith. Maybe I could just tell Chloe what to say, and she could do it. Don't you think she would be better at it than me?"

"Would I prefer to have my church headed by a natural-born showman with a talent for bullshitting the rubes, rather than a sex-obsessed teenage lesbian? Well, no offense, but hell yeah! The problem is, she works for the other side. She's making millions preaching the patriarchal religion."

"Maybe I could convince her to change teams."

"Good luck with that. Well, I gotta go. There's a convention of wiccans up in Portland, and a lot of those can sense me when I'm around. I'm going to see if I can incite an orgy. Ta-ta."

Sure nuff, the guard came and said I had a guest. It was good to see Zana again.

"Alys, what started out as an idea in your brain has become a concrete reality.

"No way."

"Well, mostly brick, but yes way. That's right. I got us a building for the church. It's on Belknap in Haltom City. It's a main thoroughfare with a respectable amount of traffic. If we spruce the place up, we could do a good business. The cracker that rented it out to me tried to give me some shit, but I reminded him of the federal laws concerning discrimination."

"He didn't want to rent to a black girl?"

"I told him it was a lesbian church."

"Nice move, Sherlock."

"I didn't know it was supposed to be a big secret."

"That's all right. It is for lesbians but also for battered women, women who want equal pay, women who are afraid of male authority figures or just women who are tired of being known as 'Joe Blow's wife.' It's a *women's* church. Dang it. That reminds me. I need to find out exactly what all the tenets and sacraments and shit like that are. Lilith was just here, and I forgot to ask her."

I realized my mistake when I saw the look on Zana's face. "What I meant was, I was just thinking of all the teachings I've heard about Lilith."

"Alys, are you feeling all right? I mean, it must be stressful, being the world's greatest lesbian lover."

"Yeah, well, I've kinda put that on the back burner for now. But now that you mention it, I have an ethics question for you. If I really like your sister and hope to have a romantic relationship with her one day, is it wrong for me to pledge myself as protector to another?"

"That's quite a moral conundrum you pose. First, let me make it clear that, if you cause my sister to fall in love with you and then break her heart, a tragic, possibly fatal mishap will occur."

"Huh?"

"Secondly, I would say that, until we can return to Aristophanes's third sex, we will always be looking for our 'perfect other self.' We will never quite be satisfied with the one we are with; we will always be subconsciously comparing them to the one in our memory.

"When you are fighting off dragons for the demure damsel you're protecting, you might resent the strong independence of the cop you love. When my sister amazes you with her courage and strength, you will find your whiny, weak little maiden less attractive.

"In short, Zeus has punished humans for our insolence to the gods by cutting us in half, and as a result, 'I can't get no satisfaction.'[2] Get it?"

"So, I can go ahead and date them both, right?"

"Alys, you're thick as a brick."

Random House came through with the million dollars, and my bail was arranged. My attorney convinced me to spend one more night in jail so I could be converted at Chloe's "Sister Love's Traveling Salvation Show."

I didn't need Chloe's money now, but I thought I might do it just for a lark. I sat in the audience and listened to her sermon. It went like this:

---

[2] Rolling Stones

"Friends, God loves you and will forgive all your sins, no matter how heinous. You know you've done terrible things, but God will forgive anything as long as you accept Jesus Christ as your personal savior.

"Don't hesitate, though. Oh, I know you're thinking, *I'll do it tomorrow*, or *I'll do it next week*, or *I just want to go out drinking and fornicating one more time, and then, I'll give my heart to Jesus*. Well, beware, y'all! Don't make the mistake my friend Molly did.

"Molly was a sweet little girl of thirteen. She was a good girl. She had never hurt anyone. She led a blameless life. Then one night she was invited over to a sleepover with a friend. Eventually, the girl who invited her over asked her, 'Molly, have you surrendered your soul to Jesus Christ?'

"Molly's family was not religious, and Molly felt uncomfortable.

"'Molly,' the girl asked, 'will you accept Jesus Christ as your Lord and Savior?'

"Molly said, 'I don't want to decide right now, Phyllis. I'll talk it over with my parents and talk to you about it later.'

Chloe walked from one side of the stage to the other and back again, staring at us in the most frightful way. When she was in close to the camera, she stopped, and the TV camera caught the tears rolling down her cheeks. "*She never got the chance!*" Chloe sobbed.

"On her way home the next morning she was attacked by a monster of a man who raped, beat, and eventually killed her! And I hate to tell you this, but her soul *went straight to hell*!

"She was sent to an eternal hell because she had an opportunity to take Jesus as her Savior and she refused!"

(Author's note: This is actual "Southern Baptist" dogma.)

"Don't make the mistake Molly did. Don't hesitate! Give your heart to Jesus *now*! Don't wait. Life is unpredictable; don't spend an eternity in hell because you didn't act when you had the chance. Come on down the aisle right now. That's right. And you, ma'am, God bless you.

"Bring your children, too. They've done heard the message now. Their little souls are in danger until they surrender to Jesus."

The sheep were heading down the aisles in droves. I stood up and joined them. There were "elders" or "deacons" or some such shit at the front to sign you up. For 10 percent of everything you make, you're in. I walked on past those bastards and walked directly toward her.

Her security people started towards me, but she stopped them. "Do you want to give your heart to the Lord?" she asked.

I walked right up to her and grabbed the microphone out of her hand. "What about the rapist?" I asked.

She saw I had gone off message and said in her real voice, "What about the rapist? What has that got—"

"He probably raped and killed a lot of girls before he was caught, don't you think?"

"I don't know what you're talking about. It's just a story."

Everybody had frozen. I turned to the audience and said, "Years later, after cutting short the lives of innocent little girls in the most agonizing and horrifying manner, while on death row, that same rapist sees the error of his ways. He calls the preacher man and says, "Preacher, I want to ask God for forgiveness and give my heart to Jesus and take Him as my Lord and Savior."

I turn back to Chloe and say, *"According to your doctrine, where is that man today?"*

Chloe was pissed. Her face was beet red. She wanted to call me all kinds of things, but she was up here in her Goody Two-shoes role.

I felt a tiny bit sorry for her, but I pressed on. "Isn't it true that, according to your doctrine, that man is in *heaven? For eternity!*"

Chloe signaled for her security team then.

They thought four of them would be enough. A minute later, one of them was trying to staunch the flow of blood from his nose; another was staring in amazement at his broken arm; and a third was on the floor, trying to get an unconscious fourth off him.

I gripped the microphone and told the tens of thousands who were watching this, "Lilith has come to set women free from these barbaric patriarchal religions. She has ordained that a church should be built in her name and, yea, verily, we have done did it! Come see us at … Oh, shit. I can't remember where it is, but you'll find it."

CHAPTER 18

LONG LIVE THE QUEEN

Martha paid my bail and led me out the Lamar Street entrance to the Tarrant County Courthouse. "You'll get your money back as soon as those stupid charges are dropped," she said. What she meant was, "Don't skip town, or you'll lose a million bucks."

We walked a block to Martha's car in the hot July heat. I had spent two months awaiting trial because I hadn't had enough money to meet the bond. Wilma could have requested a "speedy trial," but my prospects did not look good right now. People tend to take "he had it coming" as a confession.

And since we're talking about confession, just between you and me, the only reason I wasn't publicly and strenuously denying my guilt was because I wanted to make Starr love me again. There it is. When Zana was talking her nonsense about a third sex, I was thinking about how Starr was undoubtedly my "perfect other half."

I have been trying since the spring of 1987 to go back in time and undo the kiss.

I now know that Starr walking in just as I was kissing Cathy was a set-up by my self-appointed nemesis, Amy Dudley, or whatever her name is. I'm pretty sure she's the one who killed Anthony Snowden, although I can't imagine why. Starr had given her a ride to Fort Worth; that's all. Maybe she knew the girl was psychotic when she did that. I can't think of any other reason why she would say, "It's all my fault."

I should tell the next paparazzi that bugs me that I didn't do it; and why don't you ask some chick named Amy where she was that night? I won't do that, though. I still think a rat is the lowest form of life—just barely above a rapist.

In Texas, if you leave your car parked in the sun with the windows up, it gets hot. "How hot does it get?" you ask.

If you leave a frozen TV dinner on your dash when you get to work at eight, it will be ready to eat when you get out for lunch at noon.

I was standing in the shade waiting for Martha's car to cool down when a chick with green hair and a ring in her nose gave me a Hook 'em Horns sign and said, "Lilith Rules."

I thanked her, and she said, "Did you hear your girlfriend came out of her coma?"

I didn't try to correct her about the relationship between Cathy and me. "Wow, that's incredible," I told her. "Thanks for telling me. I thought I was happy before, but now I really have something to celebrate."

I tried to get her number, but she already had a girlfriend and she implied that it was kind of tacky for me to try to hit on the person who told her about her girlfriend coming out of a coma. Well, like Ricky Nelson said, "You can't please everyone, so you got to" … You know, fuck 'em.

Martha was excited about the news, too. We decide to drive straight to the Anderson's house. We didn't even call ahead. We assumed Cathy would be glad to see us. When we got there, Mr. Anderson invited us into the living room.

"There's good news and bad," he informed us. "Cathy has awakened from her coma, but she thinks she is Catherine of Aragon." Mr. Anderson confessed that he and his wife were having a difficult time taking care of Cathy since her return from the hospital. She refused to acknowledge them as her parents.

"Don't be ridiculous, "she said. "My parents are Ferdinand and Isabella. I am the queen of England. I will *not* make up my bed."

When Cathy's mother led me into her room, Cathy called out, "Maria, where have you been?" She has apparently mistaken me for Maria de Salinas, Catherine of Aragon's lady-in-waiting for twenty years.

"Ever since Henry banished me to Kimbolten, my bed has been cold and lonely. You must join me tonight."

It was fairly common for a queen's female attendants to sleep with her in the sixteenth century, for warmth if nothing else. In order to put Cathy's troubled mind at ease, I agreed to spend the night with her. I didn't know what to expect, and I was relieved when she just wanted to talk before falling asleep. The story she told me explained a lot.

"We were both just fifteen. We didn't know what we were doing. The Europeans have a strange custom of making a public spectacle of the wedding bed. I had never seen anything like it in Spain. It was practically public copulation. Dozens of handmaidens undressed me and then stood outside the door giggling. A group of drunken, rowdy men carried Arthur to the bed and cheered him on. I was trying to hide under the covers. The men finally left the room but remained just outside the door, yelling bawdy suggestions.

The Legendary Lesbian Lothario

"It was hours before we could do anything but look, shamefaced, at each other. When it finally quieted down, we tried. I did everything I could think of. I returned his kisses passionately. When he told me to spread my legs, I spread them as far as I could. It was hopeless, though. Every time he tried to enter me, his little thing dwindled. Then he did an odd thing. He rolled me over on my stomach! Then he tried to put it … um … in the wrong hole!

"'Arthur, what are you doing?' I screamed.

"He put his hand over my mouth. I wiggled, shifted, and bucked. I had never heard of such a practice. I didn't just think it was unnatural; I thought it was impossible! Finally, he stopped trying to poke it in and just rubbed and rubbed against my bottom until I felt warm liquid squirting on to my back.

"And that was it. In the morning, Arthur acted like a complete ass (or a fifteen-year-old boy—same thing!). He cut his hand slightly and wiped the blood on the sheet. He draped the sheet over the balcony to prove he had taken my maidenhood. He shouted something boastful about being thirsty because he had been in Spain all night. The crowds cheered.

Arthur was caught in some compromising situations with other teenage boys in the following months. These were, of course, hushed up. He was found dead five months later. I believe it was by his own hand. That is why I was able, so many years later, to swear on the Bible that our marriage had never been consummated."

⁓

Zana was bugging me to make an appearance at the new church. I asked Cathy if she would consent to go along. The queen was in a benevolent mood and agreed.

It was eleven o'clock when we in arrived. In Texas, that's when the temperature goes from hot to unbearable. Cathy hurried inside of the air-conditioned building. I lingered on the scorching sidewalk to savor my first view of my new church.

It was just a rectangular brick building. The vertical "Haltom" sign looked like it had been there since the building was erected in 1941. The one cool thing about it was the large (albeit plain) marquee that proclaimed in foot-high letters, "Church of Lilith."

Zana and I were admiring the facade of the old building and trying to guess the seating capacity when there were squeal of brakes and a screech of tires and a huge *bang* from across the street.

An old pickup truck had smashed into the fruit stand across the street. The people who had been inside the fruit stand were understandably upset and were questioning the driver of the truck about his mental health. He was ignoring them. He was marching across Belknap Avenue straight toward us. He was an old, fat man with a checkered shirt and starched blue jeans with a crease in them. His belly was so distended, he resembled a pregnant woman in her ninth month.

"What's going on here?" he demanded.

"Well," Zana answered, "apparently, someone built a fruit stand in your parking space overnight."

The white-haired geezer ignored the black girl and turned toward me. "What the devil is a Church of Lilith? I've been a pastor for thirty years and I've never heard of such a thing."

"Well, you have now," I told him. "We are a church that celebrates the gospel of the return of Lilith. We are here to share the truth of what happened in the Garden of Eden. We are here to glorify the name of Adam's legitimate wife, Lilith."

The old man turned red and grabbed his chest. It's a wonder he didn't die on the spot from apoplexy (and a pity). "You're a bunch of devil-worshipping witches," Fred W. Swink declared.

He turned to the small crowd that was gathering in the street. "If they've got a negro and a hippie on the outside, what must they be hiding on the inside?" he bellowed in his best Baptist preacher voice. "How can the citizens of Haltom City accept such blasphemy in their midst? Such a thing would never happen in Riverside. We are good, clean, law-abiding, taxpaying citizens in Riverside!"

"That's code for 'white folks,'" Zana explained to me.

"I am the Reverend Fred W. Swink," he roared at me. "And I curse your church and will not rest until I see it burned to the ground." He turned to make his grand exit, but he had to stop for the traffic.

I made sure everybody in the remaining crowd could hear me as I returned a curse to him:

May the Bird of Paradise fly up your nose.

May an elephant caress you with his toes.

May your wife be plagued with runners in her hose.

May the Bird of Paradise fly up your nose."[3]

I guess I told him.

Inside the church, the queen of England introduced me to her newest subject. "Alys, this is Eleanor. She keeps her face in a jar by the door."

"I'm terribly sorry to hear that, Eleanor. If Coach Rivers were here, I'm sure she would suggest you get over yourself and adopt an orphan. Who knows? You might even get laid."

"It's for all the lonely people, Miss."

---

[3] Little Jimmy Dickens

"Of course, it is, dear. If the queen will allow it, do you suppose you could introduce me to the rest of the congregation?"

There were eleven of them in all. They weren't all as crazy as Eleanor, but there were no future influencers in there. The average age was fifty, and they all had at least three cats. There were only two young ones, and one of them was Eleanor. The other one was so obviously enthralled with the queen that I knew I had no chance, but I gave it a shot anyway. "Hi, my name is Alys. This is, in fact, my church."

"Do you know the queen?"

"Would you believe we were once intimate lovers?"

"No."

"Would you believe we were once close friends?"

"You don't really seem in the same league with her, to be honest."

"Would you believe I once prostrated myself on the ground so she wouldn't have to step in a puddle?"

"Could you introduce us?"

When the door opened to the little two-bedroom apartment in Denver, all the pieces fell into place for Nan. She knew that this petite pregnant woman, who looked so like Alys, had killed Anthony Snowden. She knew, when she excused herself later to go to this woman's bathroom, she would find a bottle of Rainbow Light Prenatal One Multivitamins. She just couldn't imagine why this Colorado resident had killed a man who, except for when he attempted to flee to Mexico, had never been out of Texas.

For the first time since she had vowed to free Alys, she relaxed. "Hi, I'm Officer Nan Butler, with the FWPD. I'm looking for Starr Williams. I was told she lived at this address."

"Hi. I'm Amy. Starr doesn't live here anymore, but come on in. Have a cup of tea. I'd love to hear why the FWPD is looking for Starr."

Tea was served and small talk was made. Then Nan said, "I'm not here in an official capacity, exactly. I'm actually on vacation. To be completely honest, I ... well, I think I'm in love with Alys."

Amy did a spit take. Tea went spraying everywhere. Amy began to cough.

Nan jumped up and began to hit her on the back. "I'm terribly sorry, Amy. I shouldn't have brought my personal feelings into this. Should I leave? Do you wish me to go?"

"No, no. I'm fine. You just totally surprised me. I've never met Alys. But what I've heard about her, I'm surprised anyone could love her. Isn't she a cold, manipulative evil witch who jealously guards her father's love and won't let him love his other children?"

"Wow, Amy. Somebody's been feeding you some shit!"

CHAPTER 19

CHLOE'S "ROAD TO DAMASCUS"

"I crashed my pickup into the fruit stand," Fred told Carl when he got to the lawnmower repair shop. "Y'all got a dadgum witches' coven right in the middle of town! Hell, it's two blocks from your business, Carl. Don't that bother you?"

"They ain't done me no harm, Dr. Swink. They keep to themselves, mostly."

"Well, we'll just see about that," Brother Swink huffed and called the mayor of Haltom City, but Gladys said he was out. "You might try the fire station," she suggested.

Fred Swink figured he knew where the mayor was, and he headed for the police station on Haltom Road. In the back, where they kept the seized weapons and drugs, he found Mayor Mondale playing poker with the fire chief, the police chief, and the head of city planning.

"Y'all got a lotta damn gall, playing cards while you got a coven of witches moved into your theater," Fred told the mayor.

"They paid first and last month's rent and signed a lease for two years," the mayor replied. "Whatcha want me to do?"

"Mike, they say Eve was Adam's second wife. Can't you arrest them for that?"

"Unfortunately, it's not against the law in the United States to peaceably assemble to worship the god of your choice."

"Not even in Texas?"

"Not even in Texas."

"Well, what are you going to do about it, then?"

"We could send them to Riverside," the fire chief suggested.

So, Fred Swink went back to Riverside and told his congregation that witches were openly worshipping Satan in Haltom City and that government officials were not doing anything about it.

"Brothers and sisters, I am marching down Belknap Street next weekend, and I'm going to cast those devil worshippers out! Come with me! And, boys, bring your shotguns; for doesn't it say in Exodus 22:18, 'Thou shalt not suffer a witch to live'? You dadgum right it does!"

I got a phone call from Zana early Sunday morning.

"We've got a situation at the church," she told me. "You gotta get down here, fast." As I was getting dressed, I called out loud, "Lilith! Lilith!"

That's the problem with that goddamn demigod. She's never around when you need her.

I drove out to the church, and before I even got out of the car, I saw the problem. Someone had removed seven of the letters from our sign. It now said:

_ _ UR_ _ _F _IL _TH

"You got me out of bed before noon on a Sunday for a bit of vandalism?" I asked Zana.

"Some of the ladies are scared and nobody knows exactly why people hate us so much. The least you can do is come in and tell the ladies what this church is supposed to be all about."

As if I knew. Still, I guessed I owed it to my congregation to tell them what I knew about Lilith and the reason for this church, so I got up behind the pulpit and tried to gather my thoughts. I was happy to see Cathy and Eleanor sitting together. They were sitting quite close and making goo-goo eyes at each other. I couldn't wait to find out the dynamics of that relationship. I was also pleased to see that all eleven (now twelve, with Cathy) of our members were present.

"Ladies," I began, "I recently discovered something you may not be aware of. I have been told, on the very best authority, that Eve was not the first wife of Adam. God, in fact, created Adam and Lilith. He created them from the clay of the earth that brings forth life in flowers and trees, in grass and grains."

What the hell was I doing waxing eloquent about something I didn't even understand? If Lilith wanted me to convince anybody, she should have got in touch with me. I decided just to lay out the facts as I understood them and hope the church still had a dozen members when I got through.

"OK. Where was I? Oh, yeah. Adam and Lilith lived happily in innocent bliss for about a thousand years or so. They would each give birth to a kid every year. So, by the time Eve showed up there were 365,000 happy, contented humans in a very large garden.

"Eve was the last survivor of a war on the planet Mars. She came staggering out of her crashed spaceship, covered head to foot in a spacesuit, and yelled at them, 'Y'all are all naked.'

"Adam looked down at his dick swinging free in the wind and said, 'By God, Lilith, we *are* naked.'

"Everybody started covering up their nakedness after that, because Eve had brought a virus from the Red Planet, a virus called shame. And it infected everyone—everyone except Lilith, that is. Lilith said, 'I don't what that thing is, but it's not going to make me start wearing leaves and shit.'

"Now, the next part Lilith explained to me, but I don't remember it so well. Somehow, by Eve's treachery, everybody started reproducing sexually. Lilith caught Adam doing it with Eve in the bushes. Now, Lilith didn't say this, but I imagine that, when Lilith saw them fucking, it was the first time Lilith had seen Eve naked. And Lilith realized that Eve had a red-hot, smokin' body. What I'm saying is, maybe she got jealous. Maybe Adam was showing more enthusiasm than he had with Lilith.

"Now, Adam and Eve say that God threw Lilith out of the garden. Well, they would say that, wouldn't they? Maybe it wasn't like that at all. Maybe Lilith got upset when she saw the two of them going at it. Maybe she felt the way Starr felt when she saw me kissing Cathy. Maybe her heart was broken, and she felt she had to get away for a while. Maybe if Adam had gone after her, she would have changed her mind, and they would have kissed and make up. But I, goddamn it, *Adam* was too big a chickenshit to go after her even though it was only eight hundred miles...The door of the church was slammed open and everyone turned to see Chloe standing in her little white dress and cowboy boots and yelling, *"Who's a girl gotta blow to get saved around here?"*

Eirene assured me Chloe didn't really know what that meant. "She's just precocious. She uses phrases she hears older kids use."

"The thing is," she said, when we were all three sitting in the privacy of the church's office, "we're about to lose the Will Rogers deal and the radio broadcasts. Your 'outburst' on the prison show has us losing members by the hundreds. Chloe has an idea she would like to discuss with you. I've made her promise to be on her best behavior."

And, in her very best-behaved manner, Chloe began. "For your information, smart-ass, my job is to sell a product. I do not make the product; I do not endorse the product; I just keep the rubes paying admission for the show. Eirene and her carpet muncher, Aggie, write the scripts—"

"Get out of my office."

"*What?*"

"You heard me, you rotten little prima donna. Either apologize to Ms. Worthythingy or get out. I'm a lesbian, and I will not listen to slurs against women."

"Hey, chill dude, I was just joking around."

I stood and took a step toward the girl.

"OK. OK. Eirene, I'm sorry. You know I love Aggie and you. I just don't like this one—" She turned and addressed me. "I just don't like you getting all up on your high horse about me giving speeches about things I really don't know anything about. Don't you do the same thing? You get up and make speeches about how mistreated Lilith was, but what do you really know about her? Did you know she fucked a snake?"

"*Chloe!*"

"Sorry, 'intercoursed' a snake."

"*Had* intercourse with—"

"Stop it you two," I said, exasperated. "She didn't *do* that, no matter how you say it. Don't you see, little preacher girl? That's why I have to speak out and defend her—to protect her from the lies that Eve has been spreading about her. I have to defend her because she is unable to defend herself."

"Like me," a voice from the door declared. The door opened up, revealing little Evie Whitebread.

"Evie!"

I ran to her and hugged her tight. Still holding her, I looked at Eirene and told her, "I have some idea what your little evangelist is planning. I'll need some time to think about it. You must make her understand that some of what she preaches for Lilith will be as disliked as that hateful patriarchal bullshit she was espousing."

"I never espoused—"

I ignored the little guttersnipe and continued, "Right now, I must ask you to leave. I have to get caught up with this girl, who's been on my mind every minute since I was released."

They left, and I said, "Tell me everything."

"Within an hour after you left, your lawyer, Kunsler, had put up my bail. She gave me a little money and said I was free to go. Then I realized I had nowhere to go. I said some things to my parents when I ran off with my boyfriend that I don't think they can ever forgive me for. I know I can't forgive myself. I can never go back to him, of course. He would have me selling drugs again (if not myself). I used the money Wilma Kunsler gave me to get a motel room last night, but I have nowhere else to go. I came here to beg you to let me be your ward. I can cook and clean. I can do any kind of work you want, but what I'd really like to do," she whispered as she licked my ear, "is to be your concubine. What do you say, mademoiselle?"

She sat down on a chair and crossed her legs like a man, revealing that she wore nothing underneath her dress. "See anything you like?" she asked with a saucy wink. She stood and leaned over my desk.

She raised her dress until her ass was bare. "In other words," she said, smiling, "could I be your bitch?"

I felt the sense of oppression I had been carrying around lifting. Finally, someone *got* me! Finally, there was someone else who understood that life should be full of fun and play and lots of hot, steamy sex.

"Oh, yes," I said to myself, to paraphrase Prince Arthur, "tonight I will be in France!"

You could have knocked me over with a French tickler when I realized something was holding me back. And then I realized it was Nan. It was the thought of sweet, good Nan that was blocking me from being me— trusting, honest Nan who was in love with me and hoped I wouldn't break her heart. I thought about Starr, and how I always wished I could go back and do it over again.

Maybe this was my opportunity to change my fate. I cursed my tongue even as I said, "Evie, I—"

Suddenly, the lights in my office began to flash on and off.

"Oh, shit," I said and covered my face with my hand. "You'd better go, Evie. Here, here are the keys to my mom's house. I haven't got a place of my own yet. Go there and wait for me."

"But what is it, Alys? Oh, my dear heavens, I've read the—how do you say?—situation wrong. There is someone else, non?"

"No. Not someone else. It's just Lilith."

I had said her name in the heat of the moment. I saw in my own mind Nan as a wife and Evie as a red, hot mistress who I'd vowed to protect. I was trying to reconcile that chauvinistic contradiction, and in my confusion, I had blurted out Lilith's name.

Evie's eyes widened in horror. "Lilith? Lilith is coming here? I have to get out of here!"

As she ran past me, she said, "Don't listen to her, Alys. She is the world's oldest and biggest liar. She is a master manipulator. And she's dangerous," she screamed as she ran out the door. "She can cast you into darkness and curse you to a thousand lifetimes as a cockroach."

I thought she was gone. Then she stuck her head in the door and said, "Please! Whatever you do, don't tell her about me!"

I felt Lilith's presence before she spoke. I could tell she was in a good mood. "So, how's it going, Don Juanita? You getting any?"

"I haven't had any actual sex since the last time we met, although I did feel lust in my heart a little while ago."

"Lust in your heart. Ha. You sound like the old peanut farmer, Jimmy Carter. Hey, I can make you irresistible. But if you can't close the deal, that's not my fault. OK. Enough chitchat about your boring love life. Have you struck a deal with Chloe, yet?"

"I think so. She, I take it, is going to convert to Church of Lilith and raise our visibility. We'll have thousands of members from the Will Roger's gig and tens of thousands more on the AM radio shows."

"Right. So, why so glum?"

"What if we went a different way? What if we kept it exclusive, almost secret? Wouldn't the trend-setters be fighting to get in on the newest thing?"

"Kid, I've waited five thousand lifetimes for this moment, and I have the wisdom of the ages behind me when I say this:

"Go Big or go home."

CHAPTER 20

THE CHILDREN'S CRUSADE

At 10:17 a.m. Gladys Pinkersly at the Haltom City Police Station got a call from the Church of Lilith.

Hello? This is Eleanor Digby. I'm calling from the new church on Belknap Street. It's in the building that used to be the Haltom Theater.

"What can I do for you, ma'am?"

"Well, me and Pam and some of the other girls were planning on having our inaugural meeting of the Cross-Stitch Club today in the new building."

"Uh-huh."

"Well, there's a big crowd outside and a big fat man is saying mean things about us."

"Ma'am, there is such a thing as free speech in this country."

"Well, that's what I said. But then about ten minutes ago, some of those teenage boys started throwing rocks at the marquee. The fat man's not doing anything to stop them. In fact, he's laughing at what they're trying to do."

"And what's that, ma'am?"

"Well, they've already knocked out some letters on the marquee. Now, they're rearranging them to spell obscenities.

"Wow. Tommy Henderson must be out there. None of them other boys can spell that well."

"Well, I just wondered if you could send a police car out here to run those boys off?"

"Lady, I'm sorry, but the Chief got word this morning of a slew of snipes up on Wautauga Boulevard. I'm afraid every available police unit is on a snipe hunt. Have a nice day!"

Brother Swink's "Crusade against Babylon" started out with just a few faithful members of his congregation. He had unwisely chosen a Saturday morning to make his march on the witches of Haltom City. Most of the moms and dads from his church were at Bubba's peewee football game or Sissy's soccer game … or both. When they were passing Beach Street, however, a curious ice cream truck driver started following them to see what event they were going to. His constant (and extremely loud) rendition of "Life Is but a Dream" attracted more kids. By the time they got to Beach Street, the crusaders numbered nearly one hundred (mostly kids on bikes with a sweet tooth). By the time the riot broke out that afternoon, the pimply-faced DJ for KLRD Radio 1060's "Breaking News" was calling it, "The Children's Crusade."

Consciously or not, Brother Swink used a lot of suggestive words in his condemnation of the Church of Lilith. He said that "the whores of Babylon were licentious, lewd, and lustful."

"And de-lovely," one wag yelled.

"They want to tempt our young men into carnal knowledge of their young, lithe bodies," Swink said.

Older boys, who had been sent to find little brothers and sister, began to get interested in Brother Swink's sermon.

"How exactly will they tempt us?" one asked.

"Would we need to make an appointment?" another wanted to know. "How much do they charge?"

A young girl, still in her soccer uniform, had an even larger audience than Brother Swink.

"A real witch, she said, "will have the mark of the devil on her body. The only way to tell if they are real witches is to strip them naked."

Her friends shrieked in mock horror, and the boys hooted.

"Sometimes," she yelled over the noise, "it's a third titty!"

I was watching the mob from a small window on the second floor of the theater. They were becoming rowdier by the minute. The fat man egged them on. Lilith had left on some "urgent business" without giving me any ideas on how to handle this. Dad always told me to pick out the biggest bully and punch him in the nose. I decided the only thing to do was walk out there and punch the fat man in the nose.

As I went down the stairs, I saw Chloe and Eirene.

"Y'all still here?" I asked, rhetorically.

"This is my church now, which makes this my fight," Chloe said.

The thing the soccer girl had said gave me an idea. "Eleanor, find me a marker!"

Two minutes later, Eleanor handed me a marker.

"Red? That's all you got? Red?"

"Draw a dick on me right under my belly button," I instructed Chloe.

When she had finished, I inspected her work.

"No! Not a dangling dick. I wanted the side view of a hard-on. Like this." And I proceeded to draw a proper dick on Chloe's belly.

"Now pretend to tear my clothes off and let's show these bitches some witches." With that, I ripped Chloe's shirt as hard as could and tore a good piece off. Then we ran out into the middle of the crowd saying, "She's a witch!"

"She's got the sign of the devil!"

"*You're* the witch!"

"Look! Look at the mark!"

Chloe seemed determined to tear my shorts off, too, which wasn't necessary and would be really embarrassing because I was going commando that day. To avoid her, I jumped on the hood of a car. Cars were lined up all up and down Belknap all the way to the Griff's on the corner. They were parked close enough that I could run from hood to hood to escape Chloe. I was running so fast that I couldn't stop when I got to the hood Brother Swink was standing on, preaching. He was facing the entrance to the theater. He turned around and stared at me with such a stupid look on his face I couldn't help laughing.

If I had it to do over, I would have twirled around in the air once I'd hit him so I would have taken the brunt of the fall. As it was, I landed smack-dab on top of the old man, and we hit kinda hard. When I got up, he didn't move.

"Goddamn! You've kilt him!" Chloe said, and then she pulled my shorts down around my ankles and took off running.

I stumbled after her but fell to the ground. I lay there, shorts around my ankles, knees spread wide, pudendum exposed. The boys looked between my legs hungrily (some of the girls, too!). For some reason, I thought of Shirley Jackson's *The Lottery*.

Suddenly, Nan Butler stood there, arms akimbo, with a big, red 'A' on her chest, and a red cape blowing in the wind. (Well, she WAS standing there. I had just had a bump to the head, so maybe some of the stuff I tell you isn't accurate. I'm not omniscient, you know.)

"Get back, all of you. Somebody cover her up, for Christ's sake."

"She killed the Preacher!"

Nan reached for her sidearm. Before she could start shooting people, her police car came swerving up to us, sirens shrieking and lights flashing, and the passenger door was flung open.

"Get in," Chloe yelled. Eleanor and Cathy were in the back seat mooning everybody. "Sorry," I said, and pushed Nan into the crowd. I jumped in and we sped off.

~*~

A week after the riot at the Church of Lilith in Haltom City, a meeting took place between Celeste Worthinghampton (Eirene's evil aunt and prominent Militant Feminist) and the leader of the Dianic Wiccan Church, Zsa Zsa Bosnia.

"It's time for witches to regain the respect (in other words, fear) of the people. For too long we have been represented as ugly, green-skinned hags with moles on our noses. We have been depicted riding brooms across the sky in hats that look like traffic cones. Enough!

Your church, The Dianic Wiccan church has provided respectability to witches. The only problem is that your church is too small and unknown to make witches a force again in the modern world.

"Right now, the Church of Lilith is the fastest growing religion in the country. It is a tiny denomination that believes Adam's mate was Lilith rather than Eve and that the two humans were formed with the same mud or clay or whatever. Their only scholarly source is an obscure one—*The Alphabet of Ben Sira*, which is supposedly part of the Dead Sea Scrolls.

"The important thing about them is that they are virtually unknown, and the few that are aware of them see them as a harmless, feminist wish-fulfillment type of religion. Once we control it, The Church of Lilith will be our base, and witches will finally have a political voice. *We must act now!* The time we live in is unprecedented in human history. There is taking place a tectonic shift in human perception. The Age of the Matriarch is at hand, but men will not give up their power without a fight.

"With that child evangelist leading them, the Church of Lilith will soon grow into a powerful force.

"They are still small enough, however, for us to force a merger. I suggest to you a 'hostile takeover' of the Church of Lilith. We must act fast while that church is in disarray. The leaders of the church, Alys Loxley and Chloe Foundling, are on the lam. They think they killed a preacher named Swink. He is actually perfectly healthy, although he thinks he's Quasimodo."

～✟～

There are caves on the other side of the hill from the Worthinghampton Orphanage. That's where I was hiding out when I thought I had killed the fat man. You could have knocked me over with a harlequin romance novel when Starr walked into my cave.

"My god, Starr. It's so wonderful to see you!"

"That's Special Agent Williams to you, ma'am."

"You're a secret agent?"

"*SPECIAL* Agent. I'm an assassin for the FBI now, thanks to you.

"I'm here because certain influential powers think your pathetic little church is preaching sedition and plotting to overthrow the patriarchy."

I decided to confound my old lover by quoting some of the most romantic poetry ever written:

> You're way on top now
>
> Since you left me.
>
> You're always laughing
>
> Way down at me.[4]

"But watch out now because one of these days I'm going to be on top and you'll be down here looking up and you'll be wondering how I'm going to get up there and we'll be together for just a little while—"

"Alys?"

"Yes?"

"Shut up."

"OK."

"If you will listen to me and do what I say, you can go back to being a second-rate preacher at a tenth-rate church."

---

[4] 96 Tears? and the Mysterians

"We don't have preachers; we have priestesses," I said. I had just made this up. I was flying by the seat of my pants. "Our priestesses don't preach at our congregation. They are more like counselors, who advise and guide our members. For instance, if one of our misguided members got all bent out of shape because she *thought* she saw someone she loved kissing someone else, she would be advised to stick around and make sure of what she saw before running eight hundred miles away."

"Are you denying it?" Special Agent Williams made a move to unholster her sidearm.

"Now, now, Special Agent. I didn't say I didn't kiss Cathy. I just think you may have misunderstood my motivation."

"You wanted to get inside Cathy's pants from your first day at Handley High School."

"It was just physical with Cathy."

"It's just physical with everybody for you, Alys. You just use young girls as you go from orgasm to orgasm. You think you are God's gift to women, but "you're a punk in the gutter.""[5]

"Starr, don't hate me. I can't stand it if you hate me.

That's when Nan walked into the cave. Of course.

---

[5] "The Punk and the Godfather," Pete Townsend

CHAPTER 21

KEEP YOUR FRIENDS CLOSE

"Does it feel good to throw your weight around, Special Agent Williams?" Nan asked. "Do you really enjoy strong-arming those who love you?"

"And who are you?"

"Officer Nan Butler with the Fort Worth Police Department. I wasn't around when you left Ft. Worth in 1987, but I've just recently had a rather in-depth interview with someone you spent a year with, before you became an assassin for the FBI."

Starr looked as if she would like to comment on what Nan had said, but Nan rushed ahead. "You know, the woman you are bullying could have named you as the killer of Anthony Snowden; indeed, legally, she should have. Throwing that body off the motel balcony was a felony. Alys knew very well that she was obstructing justice, but she did it because she loved you, and at the time, she thought you had killed Anthony.

"I have since found out that it was Amy Dunnally who killed him for his part in the death of Bianca Delgado. When Amy discovered that Stanley was still enamored of Cathy Anderson, she broke it off with him, unaware that she was pregnant. She then began a torrid love affair with Bianca, which ended when Bianca was beaten and raped at the orders of Anthony Snowden. Bianca spiraled downward after that, and her life ended tragically with an overdose earlier this year.

"You, Special Agent Williams, were the one who drove Amy down here for the prom. That was why, when you found Amy beating Anthony to death with a tire iron, you said, 'It's all my fault.'"

"She has a brain tumor," Starr told me. "I never should have brought her with me. In my defense, I didn't know about her thing with Bianca. But she was not mentally stable enough to return to a place where she'd had such an unhappy relationship with Stanley." She looked at Nan and asked, "Are you going to arrest her?"

"That's what I've come to talk to Alys about. I don't think the law would be terribly hard on her considering her condition. She's pregnant, and the child will probably know her less than a year before the tumor in her brain kills her."

"Let her live the time she has left in peace," I told Nan. "The state has the burden of proof. They have to prove that Anthony wasn't dead when I threw him off the railing. If they can't, it's just littering or something. I'll take my chances."

"I thought you might say that," Nan told me. "That's why I came by to ask you first."

"How did you know where to find me?"

"Martha told me. I promised her I wouldn't try to take you in. She knows ..." Here, Nan looked uncomfortably at Starr, but carried on. "She knows how I feel about you. She knows that I wouldn't do anything to hurt you. Even" (she glanced at Starr) "if some fucking Fed turns me in for it, I'll not do anything to help your prosecution.

"I would like to know before I leave what it is that the FBI agent wants you to do."

Starr turned to me. "Very soon now," she said, "your little pissant church will merge with the Dianic Wiccan Church to form the Dianic Wiccan Church of Lilith. When that happens you just have to throw your support behind Cathy Anderson for the position of high priestess and you will be found not guilty by reason of insanity."

I replied, "You are aware, are you not, that Cathy thinks she is the queen of England?"

"I've been out of town for a while, Alys, in case you didn't know. I don't know what Cathy's up to these days, and I don't care. As long as she's the new high priestess of the Dianic Wiccan Church of Lilith, she can call herself Tinkerbell for all I care."

"You're bitter," I said.

"That's what happens, Loxley, when you have your heart torn out of your chest."

Starr left us there in the cave.

"Nan, let me explain. What you heard me saying to Starr before—"

"That's alright, Alys. I understand you. I understand exactly how things are with us, but it doesn't matter. Any amount of time that we can be together is a plus for me. I know you'll always love Starr—"

"Nan."

"No, that's all right, Alys. There's no expectation of reciprocity, no demands for your affection. I love you purely and simply, and I'll always take you as you are and never try to change you."

Those words were music to my ears. This is what I had always wanted to find. It sounded like true love.

"Are you sure you don't want me to take Amy in?"

"No. I want to stand trial. If Wilma Kunsler can get me an all-woman jury, I'd like to try out the 'he had it coming' defense.

Nan dropped me at my house. I asked her if she would like to come in. She looked past me at my mom's front door and said, "I don't think that would be a good idea."

I turned and saw Evie standing there in tight, tiny shorts and my blood-stained "peace" shirt, waving at me.

"I'm just giving her shelter and protection until she can take care of herself," I explained.

Nan leaned across the front seat and gave me a scorching hot kiss. "I love you, no matter what," she said.

⌒⁄⌒

Evie had seen the kiss that Nan gave me in the car. She immediately tried to outdo it. She held me tight and tried to give me a long, soulful kiss. I resisted.

"Hold on," I said, "What's the deal between you and Lilith? You obviously not only know of her but are also terrified of her. What's that all about?

And then, a very weird thing happened. I lost her. One second, we were in a tight embrace, discussing Lilith. The next second, she was holding up that obnoxious "just one second" finger. And then it was like watching somebody listening to their boss on the phone. She would nod her head occasionally, in silent agreement. Finally, she said, "OK, Commander," out loud, and she was back.

"Alys," she said urgently, "Look at this body. Is there anything about it you don't like?"

"No, Evie, you're perfect."

"Right? This body is everything you have ever desired—the tan, perfectly shaped legs; the firm breasts that aren't too big or too small; the blue eyes; the blonde hair. It's eighteen years old so it's legal, yet the personality that accompanies it is a young, tender vulnerable and in need of a hero. Is there a flaw in this young, hot, willing body? We even threw in an ersatz French accent. Could you ask for anything more?"

"No."

"Then why aren't we upstairs in your bed right now?" At that point Evie actually snapped her fingers as if just remembering something and said, "Oh yeah. Alys, I can do things with my tongue that even you, the Legendary Lesbian Lothario, have never dreamed of. Come on, let's go."

She began to pull me up the stairs. She was surprisingly strong, and, in truth, I wasn't resisting all that much. Sex and power are the only things that matter, and this could, quite possibly, be the best sexual experience I'd ever had. The only thing was, as I reviewed the last few minutes, I had a strong suspicion that there was something odd going on.

"*Stop.*" I couldn't think clearly, but I knew this was a pivotal point in my life. It had something to do with the way I felt about Nan, and it had a lot to do with the mistake I had made with Starr, which I could never go back and change. There was a difference, though. I thought that, if I could see the difference between how I felt about Starr and how I feel about Nan, everything would be clear.

"I'm sorry," I said to Evie. "I can't believe I'm saying this, but there may be something more important than sex."

Evie was still mad at me when we went to Mr. Worthinghampton's mansion the next day. I had refused to have sex with her because I was conflicted about Nan. She had called me a lot of names and remained in a cantankerous mood. Eirene had called me and said that her daddy (Mr. W) wanted to talk to me about the possible merger of our church with a Wiccan one.

When we arrived, Mr. W was busy. Eirene tried to make us feel at home.

She went to make some coffee. While she was gone, the phone began to ring. We listened to it ring five or six times. It seemed like it would never stop.

"Maybe they need a receptionist," Evie suggested. She picked up the phone and said, "Westinghouse Orphanage. Which kid do you want?"

"No. Of course. That's what I meant to say, Worthingthing— No, she's not here. Who is this?"

Evie took the phone away from her ear and held it at arm's length. Her mouth made a big "O," and she waved me over to listen. I put my ear next to the phone.

Evie said, "Me? I'm Eirene's new assistant. How can I help you, Your Majesty?"

I heard Cathy say, "I was hoping I could get Eirene to arrange a meeting between her father and me."

"They're right down the hall, Your Highness. Maybe you could tell me what you need from him, and I could relay the message."

I stared at Evie. I couldn't believe she was doing this.

"Well, I thought perhaps he could convince his sister, Celeste, to invite me to the secret meeting where the high priestess will be chosen."

While Evie "ummed" and "uhed," I slashed on a piece of scratch paper, "They hate each other!"

"I'm afraid they are not close siblings, Madam. It's very unlikely that he would recommend you and even more unlikely that she would take his recommendation."

"Is there nothing he can do?"

"Just one second. I'll ask."

Evie set the phone down on the table and pulled me out in the hall. "Got any ideas how I can screw her?" she asked me.

"Evie, don't you think this has gone far enough. I understand that witches take the secrecy of their 'esbat' very seriously. They might get mad."

"Who do you think should be the high priestess of the church?" Evie asked me.

"Well, obviously, Chloe thought the whole thing up, but she's not interested. And, really Evie, if the truth were told, *I* was the one who told Chloe we need a *new* god who would allow us to kill our oppressors."

"Are you telling me *you* want the job?"

"Well, I'm just saying—"

"Help me become high priestess, and I'll show you a way to go back in time."

I gawked at Evie and, finally, was able to gasp, "OK."

She ran back and picked up the phone, "Hello. Mr. W says to go disguised as Gertrude Stine. She's a famous Wiccan from Washington, well known as an iconoclast and trendsetter. Celeste has never seen her before. But if you dress in her distinctive style, she'll know you must be Gertrude."

Evie went on talking for several minutes and then hung up the phone, giggling.

"I hope you know what you're doing," I said. "I think you may have just sent poor Cathy into the lion's den."

Eleanor was persuaded to attend the Wiccan function as Gertrude Stine's personal assistant, Sylvia Path, but she was not sanguine. "Witches hate to be made fun of. They haven't been taken seriously in centuries. If they think we are playing a prank—"

But Cathy was insistent (and persuasive). And despite Eleanor's premonitions, they found themselves, a few weeks later, entering a ranch in the far western outskirts of Fort Worth. A ten-minute drive through cactus and scrub brush led them to the opulent mansion belonging to Celeste Worthinghampton, estranged (and despised) sister to Lawrence Worthinghampton.

When she entered, Cathy felt overdressed … because she was dressed. Most of the guests were naked. Some of the women were drunk and beginning to show it. Most of the men were drunk and having a good time—and proudly displaying it.

Eleanor was entirely covered in a black robe complete with cowl, but when she removed it, she was wearing a completely appropriate little red string bikini bottom.

Cathy, on the other hand, was wearing a white, polka dot party dress from the fifties, a pearl necklace, and a bouffant hairdo. This, Evie had assured her, was Gertrude Stine's idiosyncratic style of dress.

There were rivers of champagne and smokestacks of marijuana being passed around, and someone was always around making sure that Cathy and Eleanor were being served.

Except for a diamond necklace, Celeste Worthinghampton was completely naked when she sat next to Cathy and ran her hand up Cathy's dress.

"Would you like some good hashish?" she asked.

With one hand busy, Celeste needed some help to light the hash. Cathy helped willingly, with much delight. She was having the time of her life!

Many kisses later; many caresses later; many tongues, belly buttons, cunts, asses, and orgasms later, Celeste asked if she would serve as guest host.

Cathy magnanimously accepted the honor. She was carried to the altar in the center of the huge living room. Her dress had long since been removed. She was lain (or possibly laid) on the altar with her knees raised and her feet spread.

"Praise Diana," the crowd chanted.

(The thought, *This is better than being a queen*, ran through Cathy's mind and then opened the third door on the left and disappeared.)

"Let the sacred rite begin," Celeste called out, standing behind Cathy's head. Celeste was reaching out to caress Cathy's breasts, her own pendulous breasts tantalizingly close to Cathy's lips. Cathy forced her eyes away from the enticing sight to see the ceremony being enacted.

"Let the initiate worship Diana," Celeste called.

"Worship Diana, worship Diana," the crowd chanted.

Cathy saw a girl carrying a jug of wine walking slowly toward her.

(The thought, *She's the initiate, she's going to "worship" me*, ran through Cathy's mind and then threw itself down a dark stairway in despair.)

Cathy saw the girl accidentally jog the wine and spill a few drops. (It occurred to Cathy, at that precise moment that Eric Burdon and War were in the building performing their big hit, "Spill the Wine.") The girl made a silly O-mouthed face and giggled. Then she put her serious face on and continued. It suddenly occurred to Cathy that the girl was no older than Chloe.

The girl is a child, she thought, groggily. *She can't be more than elven or twelve.* "No!" she cried.

Celeste's grip went from her breasts to her shoulders. "You know the procedure, Gertrude," she hissed as she held her down.

"*No!*" Cathy willed her legs to move. She threw herself off the altar and fell to floor. She stumbled to her feet and tried to walk away.

"*Behold the false priestess!*" Celeste screamed. She grabbed Cathy by the hair and held her up straight. "She worships the false goddess, Lilith!"

"To the dungeon with her," some moron yelled out. I mean a McMansion in West Texas isn't going to have a dungeon, right?

Eleanor Digby stood at the door of the dungeon and cried out for help. Nobody came.

All those phony people, where did they all come from?

When the party's over, where *do* they all belong?

224

She listened to the string section of an orchestra come to its mournful conclusion and bowed her head.

"What was I thinking last night?" Cathy groused. "I should have known better," she said. "I should have learned from all those gang initiation movies.

"There I was, waiting for someone to ask for my signature in blood. But that's not the way it works. The gang makes you commit a crime. Then you wake up the next day, and you're already damned. I was damned lucky that girl revealed she was a minor before I did something that would damn me forever."

"Are you talking about the initiate?"

"Yes, they must have drugged her poor, sweet soul as well."

"That was Hilda. She's thirty-three.

"No shit! Man, that was good-ass hash!"

CHAPTER 22

AND YOUR ENEMIES CLOSER

Martha called an emergency meeting of the Vaginal Vigilantes. It was held at the church on Haltom Road. The guest of honor was Lawrence Worthinghampton.

"I have asked you here today because you are the last hope for humanity. A series of unfortunate events has led man (and woman) to the very precipice of extinction. Only you few, you happy few, you brave band of sisters can stop the conflagration that will soon envelope the world. She, who hath no stomach for this fight—"

"Hey, Henry V," I yelled, "Get to the point."

"OK, fine. It has been brought to my attention that a coven of witches, led by my own sister, Celeste, are planning on creating an army to make war on men."

"*Yeah*!" I cheered and then realized I'd read the room wrong. Everybody was staring at me.

"This would, obviously, be a very bad thing," Mr. W continued. "A war between men and women would negatively impact population growth."

"Yeah?" Jesus, what's wrong with these girls?

"The brave little girl that brought this to my attention has also informed me that these witches have kidnapped Cathy Anderson. The poor child that risked her life to bring me this news has suffered much lately. While serving time in the county jail, she was forced into sexual slavery by a member of this very gang, *Alys Loxley*!"

"Say what?"

"And yet, after being treated in such a depraved and humiliating way, this sad but brave orphan wants to help us. She has come up with a plan to rescue Cathy and defeat the witches. Ladies and ... well, let me present Eve Langorgeous."

"Thank you, thank you." Dressed like a young Emma Watson going to Sunday School, Evie stood there, waving shyly. "I'm embarrassed that Larry, I mean Mr. W, had to mention all that I've been through. I hate to think of all of you knowing that I had to escape from the Legendary Lecherous Lizard just this morning. I tremble in shame to think of you all knowing that just last night Alys was forcing me to lick her clitoris while I fingered her cunt and stuck another finger up her ass."

I was in shock, of course, knowing I'd been sucker punched by the kid I had thought was so innocent, but there was something worse. The hair on the back of my neck stood up as I turned around. The sense of déjà vu was overpowering as I looked at the back door and saw Nan standing there.

I jumped up, knocking my folding chair into the people behind me. "It's not true, Nan! It's a lie. I wouldn't do anything! *I never touched her*!" But I was talking to air. Nan was gone.

I hate being a pariah. I've gotten used to having young, pretty girls around me who I can talk to and flit with and like that. Another thing I'm sick of, is being hated by the girl I love. It's happened to me twice now, and it's not fair. I'm not a bad person, you know, I'm really not.

OK. I'm a murderer, and I cheated on Starr, and sometimes I argue with the umpire on close calls that I really know are out, but I'm a good daughter. I defended my dad when people called him a crook. Also, I didn't kill my mom when she practically let Peterskin move in. (Hell, I didn't even kill Peterskin!)

I climbed to the top of Mount Worth. "Mount Worth" is what I call the hill where both the Worthinghampton summer cottage and the Worthinghampton Orphanage are. I yelled at the top of my lungs, "*Lilith!*"

I took a flask out of a back pocket in my jeans. I took a shot of Gilbey's Gin. "*Lilith!*" I screamed. I sat down on a rock and took another swig.

"I can see why you're not a more popular demigod," I said in a more conversational tone. "You are never around when you're needed. Right now, I need you to tell me why I'm such a loser. This kind of thing shouldn't even happen once to somebody, much less twice."

I imbibed another swallow. "It's been a year-and-a-half since I tried to give Cathy a big ol' slobbery kiss, and I've thought about it every day since. That kiss was only partly a culmination of my adolescent dreams. Sure, you see a girl like that, and you know that, in a real world, your lips will never touch that girl's luscious lips. But you can't help but think that, somewhere deep inside, you're special—that, in some dream realm, you have superpowers that make you desirable to the Cathy Andersons of the world. Of course, that was one thing that drew me to her that night.

"But I've begun to think that there was something more. I suspect that, in that swamp of hormones and dreams that is my mind, I secretly wanted to escape the chains of my relationship with Starr. I think I felt trapped. I felt *married*!

"There! Goddamn it, I've said it. I felt that Starr was tying me down. I felt like I was her prized possession, and she would not let go of me.

"Oh, god, Lilith! Do you have any idea how that makes me feel?

"Shitty? Stupid?"

"*Fuck*!" I dropped the flask and spilled a lot of the priceless nectar. "Don't do that!"

"Sorry. There were no lights to flash on and off."

"So, tell me, oh wise one, am I not being unfairly cursed to have lost my one true love twice?"

"Alys, I'm no good at being noble, but it doesn't take much to see that the problems of three little people don't amount to a hill of beans in this crazy world."

"Oh my god! You've existed on this planet for over five thousand years, and all you got for me is Rick from *Casablanca*?"

"How about, 'Get over yourself'!"

"Who said that?"

"*I* did, you drunken degenerate. Stop feeling sorry for yourself and go build me a church."

"Done and done, Your Lordship. It's on the corner of Belknap and Denton Highway—right in front of the blood donation center."

"No, you big dunce. I need you to turn that old ramshackle building into the biggest church since Peter started the Catholic Church. Chloe is doing a great job of making converts. Now I need you to write my Fifty-Five Tenets and nail it to the door of Saint Basilica's Cathedral."

"Would First Methodist down on Hemphill do? I'm just saying, I'm beat. I feel like I've been tied to the whipping post. That Eve Langorgeous sure played me for a fool. She seems like a weak, helpless little kitten, but she's a master manipulator and a goddamn liar."

"Haven't you guessed who she is? What's puzzling you is the nature of her game. (Oh, yeah.)"

I can't actually see Lilith, so I don't know exactly what she was doing for the next few minutes, but I strongly suspect she was dancing. I heard her say, "Get down with it," and very faintly, "What's my name? You're to blame."

Then she was breathing hard and kinda wheezed, "I can't boogie like I did five thousand years ago."

"You're saying that little Evie Langoreous is the same Eve that had you out of the garden all those years ago?"

"Ha! Wait until you get to number fifty-five! You have no idea of the evil that girl is capable of. You want to know what *really* happened in the Garden of Eden? OK, I'll tell you. Adam and a bunch of the boys went off to play ball. Eve and I were bathing in the pristine waters of the pond.

"It was Eve who started it. I had always thought of sex as a bodily function used strictly for reproduction. Eve told me that, on Mars, the wives of soldiers had learned ways of amusing themselves when their husbands were off to war. She demonstrated. I was hooked immediately. I never had known that sex could be so pleasurable and fun. We scissored blissfully all afternoon long.

Then, when we heard the men returning, Eve got scared. She was afraid I would tell Adam what we had done. I hadn't realized that the virus she had brought to Earth from Mars was so virulent. Shame was an inexplicable and toxic virus, and Eve had it bad. In a fit of remorse and fear, she slew me."

"She slew you?"

"Yeah. That's the word they made up for it later when the whole Cain and Abel thing happened. We had never seen death before, and none of us understood it. Eve stood there with the tree limb in her hand saying, 'Get up, Lilith.' And I was standing there trying

232

to get Eve to listen to me and wondering what that lump of flesh on the ground was.

When the men approached, Eve kicked some leaves over my body.

"'Lilith?' she answered. 'No, I don't see Lilith around anywhere. You don't see her, do you?'

"I was standing there, yelling and cursing and waving my arms around; but none of them saw me. No one has seen me ever since. Until I found you, nobody has heard me, either."

CHAPTER 23

THE RESCUE OF CATHY ANDERSON

The Church of Lilith had over eighty thousand members in 1989, but most of them were "radio members." They listened to Chloe on the radio and sent their tithes to an address that turned out to be the Worthinghampton Orphanage. There was only one brick-and-mortar church in those early days, and it was overseen by Zana Butler.

(Of course, as the years passed, the churches grew like mushrooms. Recently, General Scovall was quoted as saying, "One can hardly fire a Howitzer these days without hitting a Church of Lilith.")

Zana was sitting in her office when Penelope Porterman knocked tentatively on her door. "Come in."

"Ms. Butler, I've found something I think you should see. I was moving the jar by the door where Eleanor keeps her face. (I thought it could use a bit more sun). I found this note, and I think it could be important." She handed the note to Zana.

To Whom It May Concern:

I feel a great deal of trepidation about our upcoming visit with Celeste Worthinghampton. We are going in disguise, and Celeste doesn't know us. Cathy thinks it's funny, but I do not. I am not sanguine about the reaction of the Wiccans if they find out we have crashed their party. It is also a secret ceremony called an esbat. They could be quite angry. If we should disappear, please look for us at Celeste's mansion in the Tanglewood neighborhood out by Hulen Street. Thank you.

P.S. Somebody water the aspidistra.

Zana sent the note to me, and I immediately called Nan. Nan wouldn't take my call, so I called Starr.

"What do you want?" she asked me.

"Mr. W's evil sister has kidnapped Cathy and is holding her in an underground dungeon."

"Aren't all dungeon's underground?"

"Come on, Starr. Get serious. I know you cared for Cathy a bit. Won't you help me save her for old times' sake—for what we once had?"

"*Oh. My. God.* I don't believe you! Your name should be Echo. Can't you stop loving your own reflection for a second and see reality? It's always been Cathy and me. I fell for her the first time I saw her cheering for Handley when I was attending Carter/Riverside. That's why I switched schools. By the time Cathy and I got to know each other, I was already going with you. I wouldn't betray you because I didn't want to be a cheater!

"Even after I caught you cheating and left town, it was *still* Cathy and me. Didn't it seem strange to you, in the summer of '87, that Cathy would cry out *my* name every time you made her climax?"

"You know, now that you mention it—"

"Alys, I tried to be a loyal and faithful partner when we were together, but the more popular you got, the more of a heartless cheater you became. So, yes, I'll rescue Cathy. But in the meantime, I sing this song to you."

To my amazement, Starr suddenly had ponytails and bobby socks. She started doing the twist and singing:

> Haven't you heard
>
> About the girl
>
> Known as the cheater.
>
> She'll take your girl and then she'll lie
>
> And she'll mistreat her
>
> It seems every day now
>
> You hear people say now
>
> Look out for the cheater
>
> Make way for the fool hearted clown
>
> Look out for the cheater
>
> She's going to build you up
>
> to let you down![6]

Well, I didn't have to take that kind of abuse from my bitter ex. I called Chloe and told her about Cathy.

"Don't care," she told me. "Do you know how many new Dianic Wiccan churches there are in Texas now?"

I told her I did not. And I was going to tell her that I didn't think that had anything to do with the main point, but she interrupted me

---

[6] "The Cheater," Bob Kuban

by shouting, "*Three*! Three goddamn Wiccan churches, and we still just have the one. That's supposed to be your side of the business. Do you have any ideas, Billy Graham?"

"I was thinking along the lines of a nice car wash—"

"*Arrgh!*"

⌘

Zana called me back and said that Mr. W wanted to see me. He insisted on meeting me at his office in downtown Dallas. Like most people from Fort Worth, I hated going to Dallas. Amon Carter famously took a sack lunch every time he had to go into Dallas, so he wouldn't have to spend any money in Dallas. People in Dallas are undeservedly snooty just because they have a larger population and few more skyscrapers than we do. They, each and every one of them, learned their driving etiquette from someone in New York.

I was looking out the penthouse window down at the Schoolbook Depository Building in Dealey Plaza.

"There's where y'all shot Kennedy," I told him when he walked in.

Like most Dallasites, Mr. W had long since gotten used to being held responsible for the assassination of JFK. He showed no reaction. I, on the other hand, had a strong reaction when I saw who followed him in.

You could have knocked me over with a pint-sized Lolita when I saw Evie come in, two steps behind him, like a well-trained geisha. When he sat at his desk, she stood behind and slightly to the right of him.

"Alys, it's good of you to have come. Eirene says howdy." (Eirene has never said howdy in her life.)

"As you know, Cathy Anderson has disappeared. All indications are that my despicable sister, Celeste, is behind her disappearance."

Behind him, Evie pointed at him and held up her index finger about an inch away from her thumb. I believe she was telling me that he had a small dick.

"How would you know?" I asked sarcastically.

Mr. W was taken aback at my apparent rudeness. "Well, we know she rented a limo that dropped her off at my sister's westside mansion. There was also a note from someone named Eleanor—"

"I'm sure you are right, sir. It was no doubt your sister who grabbed her. You don't need to worry about it, though. Starr Williams is going to rescue her."

"*No!*" Evie had taken two steps forward and slammed her hands on W's desk. "Williams is FBI, and the FBI always works for the status quo, meaning the patriarchy.

I looked at the surprised look on W's face, and instantly, I figured out her game.

I had come across it in my ventures intoBDSM Evie was an expert at playing the game called "topping from the bottom." She had done the same thing with me. She's all submissive and docile and dependent, until you realize—*she's pulling all the strings*!

"Listen," she said to me, apparently taking over the meeting, "Larry's written a note to his sister, introducing me as Cathy Anderson. She has only seen Cathy when Cathy was disguised as Gertrude Stine. As the ersatz Cathy, I can infiltrate the Wiccans and find out what their plans are."

"And find Cathy Anderson," W added, not realizing he was no longer a factor.

"I'm going with you." I said.

"The fuck you are."

"I know Cathy Anderson (and I mean that in the biblical sense). If Celeste suspects anything and tries to trip you up, I'll be there to set her straight."

(For just a second, the Jackson 5 were singing "I'll Be There." But these are serious times, and I must concentrate.)

"Why should Celeste Worthinghampton accept you as an expert on all things 'Cathy'?" Evie wanted to know.

"Don't be stupid," I scoffed. "Every lesbian in North Texas knows about the crazy time Cathy and I had in the summer of '87."

"My sister's a lesbian?"

※

Starr's plan was so meticulous and based so much on split-second timing that it took a few weeks to prepare. Evie and I, on the other hand, were in there the next day.

Evie was loving it. She felt right at home with the opulence of Celeste's mansion.

"I was born to live like this," she told me. She knew her place, though. When Celeste winked and led her off to bed, she went quietly, like a lamb to slaughter. She looked back at me when they reached the bedroom door. She widened her eyes and made an exaggerated gulp. She even started to cross herself before Celeste grabbed her ass and pulled her in.

"It wasn't that bad," she told me the next day. "She was making me feel pretty good until it just stopped, and I looked down and saw that she had fallen asleep."

Thus, the pratfalls of having a sixty-year-old lover!

While Evie was taking one for the team (so to speak), I was exploring the mansion in hopes of finding some clue as to where they might have hidden Cathy. I didn't come up with anything conclusive, although there was one thing that aroused my suspicions. There was a small door in the stairwell in the main hallway that typically would hold a broom closet or serve some such prosaic purpose. My Poirot-like instincts were aroused by the two massive military men with machine guns maintaining vigilance with a menacing mien.

Still, I found no sign of Cathy, and I wondered how long Evie could keep up the charade of being Cathy. I was wandering around the mansion, opening random doors to see if Cathy was behind one of them, when I saw Evie leaving Celeste's room. I started to walk up to her and tease her about her geriatric "sugar momma" when she took one of those new-fangled cellular phones out of her pocket. I heard her say, "Q, this is E. I'm in with the Wiccans. They think I'm C. Tell that old horndog W that they have agreed to accept Cathy Anderson (me) as the new high priestess of the Dianic Wiccan Church of Lilith. When they crown me, I will throw my support to the men of the world, and things will be as they were meant to be since I landed on earth from my home on Mars."

Then she laughed like Boris Karloff (bwa-ha-ha) and exited stage left.

Cathy and Eleanor were thrown to their knees and their blindfolds removed.

Behind a long table, seven witches sat in judgment. The one in the middle spoke, "You have been charged with falsifying your identities to gain access to a secret meeting of witches. If you tell the truth, you'll simply be banished from the Wiccans for life. If you lie, it will go hard on you. Now, who are you?"

Cathy stood. "I am Catherine of Aragon. When my husband finds out how you have treated the queen of England, you'll all be beheaded.

The witches all began to talk among themselves. The one on the end yelled back to someone who stood offstage, "It's as you said. She mocks the court."

"What is this," Eleanor cried, "some kind of witch hunt?"

"Since you will not be truthful, we will not waste any more time," the central witch declared.

"Where are the kangaroos?" Eleanor yelled sarcastically.

"We will send you to the Grand High Inquisitor—let her sort out the truth."

"*You can't handle the truth!*" Eleanor screamed.

Walking out to center stage, Evie said, "Nice Nicholson."

Evie demanded the other witches give them some privacy. She looked at Cathy and said, "Your Majesty, if you refer to me as Cathy, I'll have you back to Henry in no time."

"Thank you, witch. Can you do something about that bitch Anne Boleyn?"

"Don't worry about it. I know a French specialist who will remove her head." Evie looked at Eleanor. "You got a problem with that?"

Celeste called for Cathy and Eleanor to be released from their cell and brought to her.

"You!" she demanded of Eleanor. "Who the fuck are you?"

"I'm Eleanor. I keep my face in a jar by the door in the night."

Yeah. Well, I'm sorry to hear that, Eleanor. Now, listen. I'm going to give you two choices, OK?"

"O—"

"Don't speak. Choice one is I kill you, along with your lover here."

"What lover?"

"Choice two is you tell me this isn't Cathy Anderson, and you can go back to your face that you keep in a jar. You don't darn your socks in the night when there's nobody there, do you?"

"No ma'am, that's Father McKenzie. As far as this stranger standing next to me, I have no idea who she is."

"You had sex with her, didn't you?"

"Doesn't mean I know her."

"Good point. Well, now you know where all the lonely people come from."

"What? I don't get it."

"The 'lonely people' are people who betrayed the ones they said they loved, and are, therefore, alone."

As Eleanor went somewhere to feel sorry for herself, Celeste said to Cathy, "If you are Cathy Anderson, who have I been sleeping with?"

Starr had the whole caper planned out like a *Mission: Impossible* episode or a real-life snatch, like the elimination of bin Laden. She and Eirene and Aggie and Martha were dressed up like an all-female lawn crew. They had some pretty green uniforms that featured flimsy T-shirts and tight shorts. They drove up in a van that said "Lawn Munchers" on the side.

The security unit was not particularly suspicious of them. They knew that Celeste Worthinghampton was an eccentric old lesbian, and this seemed just the sort of thing she would do.

I joined them in the back, where they were unloading lawn equipment.

"Why don't you stay out here by the van with Eirene?" Starr suggested, "You've always struck me as more of a lover than a fighter."

"I can do both."

"Yeah, probably both at the same time."

I was still thinking of a sarcastic comeback when Starr kicked down the basement door.

"Hey, the entrance to the dungeon is under the stairs," I informed her.

"There's more than one way in," Starr replied as she nonchalantly shot a guard with a stun gun. "Martha's going in from the house, and we'll meet in the middle."

We fought our way through a long corridor and through a metal door. In the room that held the dungeon, there were all kinds of torture devices. There was a cage, but the door was open, and there was nobody inside. Starr went to the one remaining door and put her ear to it. Then she stood back and shook her head in disgust. She welcomed me to open the door, which I did.

A female guard was hastily dressing. Evie lay on the bed, not even trying to conceal her nakedness.

"Can you believe the queen of England sold me down the river?"

I don't know how they feel about it in the Navy SEALs, but it seems to me you can't abort a rescue mission just because you have the wrong hostage. Everything is on a timetable.

"Let's just take her back to Mr. W," I suggested, "and say, 'Hey, here's Cathy. See you later. Bye!'"

"Let's storm the house!" Aggie said. "We can go from room to room, busting down doors and yelling, 'Clear,' until we find her."

"They have real guns," Eirene pointed out.

That nixed that idea.

"Fuck it," Starr said. "Let's cut our losses and get the fuck out of here."

"Hey, listen," Evie said. "It's important that I'm elected high priestess. I'm here on a mission. If you allow Cathy Anderson to become high priestess, she'll simply be Celeste's goon.

"Celeste has this plan called 'helter-skelter.' The idea is to start a huge world war between men and women that will destroy civilization as we know it and bring anarchy. Cathy hopes to send the human race back to a time of kings and queens."

Starr was looking at me. "You going to let them get away with that, Loxley?"

"Hell, no!"

"Good! Then I nominate you for the office of high priestess of the Dianic Wiccan Church of Lilith."

CHAPTER 24

HOSTILE TAKEOVER

At this point, the lights began to flash on and off like crazy.

"Looks like they have some kind of electrical problem," Starr observed.

"Folks," I announced, "Evie and I are going to need the room. Can we clear the room, please?"

When everybody else had left, I opened my mouth, and Lilith began to speak. "Hello, Eve. Why is it every time I see you, you're trying to hide your nakedness? Do you remember the first time? You were giving Adam a blow job, and when I caught you, you tried to cover yourself with a fig leaf."

"I didn't know that, when I hit you with that tree limb, you would die. We didn't even know what death was then."

"Do you know the difference between karmic law and the laws of gods, Evie?"

When Evie looked confused, Lilith answered for her, "No, Eve, you do not. That's why, with each new life, you fancy yourself still in the garden. It seems bigger and noisier and more confusing each time, but you still think you are in the garden. and it's all about you.

"Karmic law is as immutable as gravity. You cannot escape it. The laws of the anthropomorphic gods are as whimsical as a pretty girl's dance card. Gods do not make people in their image; people make gods in *their* image.

"When you were overcome with shame, fear, and anger and killed me, you won! For the following ten thousand years, the world was seen as a place where the strength and calm of the male was necessary to rule. And behind every successful man was a woman—pushing!"

"What are you going to do to me?"

"I'm going to give you a gift. I am going to give you insight into who you really are."

It was all too much for Evie. She crumpled up like a poorly written sheet of paper in a lousy manuscript. When she finally pulled her head out of her ass, her eyes were all googly and crazy, and she said:

I'm the guy in the sky

Flying high

Flashing eyes

No surprise I told lies

I'm a punk in the gutter

I'm the new president

But I grew and I bent

Don't you know? don't it show?

I'm the punk with the stutter.[7]

"Call your dogs off," Celeste told her brother, "Cathy Anderson is here of her own free will and wishes to serve as high priestess. Here, hold on, I'll see if she will deign to talk to you. Your Majesty? My brother, the grandson of the Earl of Wappan, asks if you are comfortable here at my humble abode.

"Yeash? This is your queen speaking. My accommodations are quite adequate, but I find it dashed hard to get a hold of my husband, the king. You know the fellow—fat, ruddy beard, always bothering the serving girls. If you see him, tell him it's quite cold at Kimbolten, and I could do with some more blankets. Right then. Cheerio!"

"Celeste? Celeste!"

"I'm back, brother."

---

[7] "The Punk and the Godfather," the Who

"What have you done with Evie? You didn't hurt her, did you?"

"*I* didn't do anything to her, Lawrence. Those Amazons you sent to 'rescue' Cathy broke her mind. She goes around talking about 'pounding stages like a clown' and 'broken glass' and 'bloody faces.' We let her wander around loose, sort of like a court jester."

"I want her back, Celeste."

"Forget about her. You've more important things to think about. I've filed papers. There will be a vote on the merger of our two churches in two weeks. The ballots will include a vote for the high priestess. Remember, a vote for Cathy Anderson is a vote for the merger. Everybody loves Cathy. You better come up with a good candidate."

Then she did what seems to be the new thing; she laughed like Boris Karloff. Bwa-ha-ha.

I was a little disappointed in the car wash. Oh, we washed a lot of cars and raised some money, but I was trying to recruit members, and the results were not encouraging.

Take Lorraine, for example (pause, pause, pause) please![8] No, but seriously, folks, Lorraine was one of the few young straight members of the church. One of the car wash customers asked her out. Nice, huh?

Except when she came to church the next day, she was all, "We need more organization. We need more leadership. We need this and that. Obvi, the guy worked for the Wiccans! If you saw Lorraine's face, you would know I'm right. There's no other reason why anyone would take her out.

And it wasn't just the young singles the witches were courting. Our three cat ladies were enthralled by the stories of Carolyn, the Collin County Cat Lady who took some of her cats to church with her.

"The Wiccan Church understands," she said. "They know that some cats get separation anxiety when Mommy has to go somewhere. They have a special room where your cat can stay, and you can go in and comfort them periodically. Does your church have anything like that?"

---

[8] Paraphrase of a Henny Youngman joke. Interestingly, this is the first joke ever told. When Adam was cast out of the garden, he went on tour telling of his experience. When he would give examples of problems in the garden, he would always say, "Take my wife ... please."

I figured Cathy and Eleanor had already gone over to the dark side. If our three cat ladies went with them, that left seven ladies who controlled the fate of Lilith's church. If two of them were seduced by the dark forces, it was all over for Lilith. And if it was all over for Lilith, she'd never let me hear the end of it!

I was so desperate I went to Chloe for help. Chloe claims to be a Communist. She says that property is theft. That may be so, but the Worthinghampton Orphanage was the only orphanage I knew of that had its own batting cage. And Chloe was the only one who used it.

She turned it off and ran to me when she saw me approaching. I held my arms out to her to catch her in a loving embrace … and she tackled me around the waist and wrestled me to the ground. She pinned my shoulders; counted to three; and jumped up, yelling, "Oh, yeah! I'm still the champ. I still got it!"

"Chloe, listen to me. This is important. The future of humanity hinges on this. I need you to deliver a sermon to our church on the importance of loyalty."

"No can do, Loxter. Zana does all the sermons at the church. I just do the radio gig now. And, in sixteen months, I'll be playing shortstop for the seventeen and under national little league team."

"No way!"

"Way, dude. Coach Wilson says I'm already better than most of the boys on the eighteen and under team. He just wants to wait and make sure I don't have any freak development like you." She looked at my tits when she said that. "Heavens forfend!"

"Heaven forfend, indeed."

"Fine, Chloe. I wish you the best of luck. I hope your titties don't get so big you can't hit a fastball. I hope your baseball career is successful. I hope you meet a nice guy (or girl) and have a loving relationship. I'll try to feel good about it for you. It's just ... well, I kinda feel like the whole weight of the world is on my shoulders lately. I've been hearing voices and" (voice cracking) "I just don't know" (tears running down cheeks) "how much longer I can take it all alone" (complete breakdown with heartfelt sobs).

"Oh, Alys! I'm so sorry" (a light, tentative touch on the shoulder).

Just as she starts to turn that touch into a sisterly hug, I jump up and shout, "Oh yeah! I still got it. I'm still the champ!"

On April 28, 1990, my trial—for a crime that had been committed almost two years before—began. I wore this cute shiny gold shirt with a beige cashmere skirt. The skirt matched the sweater I had to wear because they kept the thermostat in the courtroom set at 72. My skirt was short. The jurors could see my shapely legs. (I figured that'd get me a couple of not guilty votes.)

The details were boring to me. I mean, I was there, right? I started taking a book to read. It was called *An Instance of the Fingerpost.*[9]

"Not interested in the outcome of this case?" the judge asked me.

I looked at her and answered with all the wide-eyed innocence of a sheltered white twenty-year-old, "The two people I love the most in the world know I'm innocent. One of them will surely save me."

I was expecting Starr or Nan to save me. I had two fantastic scenarios. In one, Starr testifies that I took the blame to protect her. In the other, Officer Butler testifies that I could not have been the murderer because the timeline proved that, at the time of the murder, I was home alone, in bed with Terry Pratchett.

What I didn't expect was a pale, small-chested, very pregnant version of me waddling down the courthouse aisle to testify as a prosecution witness. Amy Dunnally had agreed to testify that, when I invited Starr and her to the prom, I vowed to kill Anthony Snowden for revealing that I had once committed a murder.

While Amy was on the stand answering her prearranged questions from the prosecution, I wrote a note to Wilma, "Ask her about our dad."

---

[9] Full disclousre: In many universes, this book was not published until 1997.

I'm not proud of that moment. It wasn't the kindest thing I could have done; but it was effective. The moment Wilma brought up our mutual dad, Amy began to lose it. When Wilma began to read a letter from my dad stating that he wished he could be there to testify as a character reference, Amy completely lost it.

"You goddamned witch," she yelled at me, "You put a spell on him and took him away from me! And then, when you saw that picture of Bianca and me on that skiing holiday, you told me Anthony was the one responsible for her death. *You* are the one who made me kill him. It's all *your* fault!"

Perry Mason, you got nothing on me.

CHAPTER 25

NOWHERE YOU CAN BE BUT WHERE YOU'RE MEANT TO BE

Before Pregnant Amy waddled in and saved my bacon, Wilma Kunsler had been going for the insanity defense. She told the jury that I heard voices. She put me on the stand and said,

"One of the voices you heard was someone called Lilith, was it not?"

"The one voice I heard was Lilith."

"And who exactly is this 'Lilith'?"

"Lilith is the first woman. She was created equal to the first man."

"And when did this happen?"

"About ten thousand years ago."

"Wow, Lilith must be getting a bit 'long in the tooth' by now."

"Your sarcasm is a result of the indoctrination you've been exposed to since you were an infant. Western culture is controlled by a religious system that counts on the fear and gullibility of the individual. Most of the world has seen the logic of reincarnation and the beauty of karma.

"If one observes nature, one sees that life is cyclic and unending. The bird singing outside your window when you awake in the morning is not the same one you heard last spring; and there is a bird singing in your yard every year."

"Are you saying that you actually believe in reincarnation?"

"Reincarnation is not something you have to believe in. It's a fact, like gravity. If you wish to close your eyes to it, do so; it makes no difference."

Saying that reincarnation is a real thing, is enough, in most juror's eyes, to make you nuts. But just to make sure, Wilma took it further. "What did Lilith say to you the first time she spoke to you?" she asked me.

"She told me I was perfectly justified in killing the man who had just raped me. She told me he had it coming. She also told me that I would get what I had coming, whether it was punishment or reward. She showed me I could live my life standing proud, without cowering on my knees to some god who threatened me with eternal damnation."

Once Amy confessed to the murder of Anthony Snowden, people started to like me again. I was invited onto Chloe's radio broadcast as a guest a few times, and that led to an invitation from one of the Wiccan churches that was planning to merge with our church. I suspected it was a setup, but Lilith was emphatic that I get her word out to these people, so I accepted.

I really hate proselytizing. It's extremely boring. Lilith has these main points that I have to keep going over and over every time I speak:

1. Lilith is the original (hence, legitimate) wife of Adam.
2. She and Adam were created as equals.
3. Eve flattered and manipulated Adam into thinking he was superior to Lilith in order to effectively control Adam.
4. Lilith was never "banned" from the garden. She was murdered by Eve and her body hidden.
5. It was Eve who introduced "shame" to the garden. What Adam and Lilith did before Eve's arrival was simple, innocent fun.

I know the first time I heard these things, I found them very interesting. But the more I repeated them, the less interested I was.

I was droning on about these points at the Highland Park Wiccan Tabernacle when one of Swink's goons came running down the aisle and threw a gallon of red paint on me. "Whore of Babylon!" he yelled at me. "The blood of the Lamb is on your hands!"

The Wiccans have good security, and the guy was whisked away while I tried to get as much of the paint off me as I could. In that interim, Lilith told me a few things I found really interesting. I decided to share them with the congregation.

"Let me clear up one thing about Lilith's relationship with Jesus of Nazareth," I said. "It's true that, in those days, Lilith still reincarnated in the traditional way—in other words, from one corporeal body to another. It is also true that Lilith was a close, personal friend of Pontius; in fact, they 'had a thing going on.' It is further true that the night before Jesus appeared before Pontius Pilate, Lilith advised him to 'wash his hands' of the whole affair, but she only did so because she thought it was important that history showed it was his own people who wanted Jesus dead, and not the government.

If the men thought their attacks on me would stifle Lilith's message, they were sorely mistaken. The more the patriarchy attacked me, the larger my audiences grew. As the time for the election grew near, it looked like I was the most popular public figure around. I let it go to my head and announced that I was "more popular than the Beatles." My hubris came back and bit me on the ass, of course. People cursed my blasphemy. They hung me in effigy. They would have burned my records if I'd ever made any.

Martha patiently explained to me that I needed to concentrate on the seven votes that could block the hostile takeover by Celeste and her witches.

I told her, "Martha, Lilith doesn't want to have a church of twelve spinsters whose idea of a good time is a cross-stitch club. Lilith wants a church that can take on the patriarchy and change the world."

Then Martha asked me how I knew what Lilith wanted, and I explained that Lilith was a non-corporeal entity who could communicate with me telepathically. Martha asked me if I had been sniffing paint fumes lately.

I didn't think anything about it until the day before the vote on the merger of the two churches. I was called to the church on Belknap Street and was amazed to see almost everyone I knew. Mr. W was there. So were Martha, Eirene, Aggie, and Chloe. My mom and Starr were there and getting along famously. But most incredibly of all, Nan was there; and she seemed happy to see me.

"Nan!" I blurted. "I'm so happy to see you. I have to tell you that I love you, and I will never cheat on you. Those things that Evie said about me were all lies. She wanted to do all those things, but the thought of you stopped me. Do you realize what this means? For the first time in my life, my true love has kept me from fucking somebody who was willing to fuck me!"

Maybe not the greatest speech to make in front of Mom and Starr—or anybody really. But it was from the heart. As the group uncomfortably moved past my opening outburst, I realized this was a "come to Jesus" meeting. Or an intervention. Or both.

"Sweetheart," Nan said, "I love you, too. So does everyone in this room. We just want to make sure that the stress hasn't been too much for you, lately. Knowing you like I do; I'm frankly surprised you have any interest in being a high priestess of a church. Maybe you need a rest."

I looked at everybody who had ever meant anything to me, and I said, "Listen, ladies, it really doesn't matter. If I'm wrong, I'm right. Where I belong, I'm right. And where I belong is right here doing what I'm doing. There's nowhere else for me to be, nothing else I should be doing. I think there are a lot of frightened, lonely souls out there who suffer from despair. They think their miserable years are numbered and that, when they are over, they will cease to exist. Someone needs to tell them that they are immortal.

"Listen people, death is only a transition. When this life is over you will live again … and again. The sort of life you will live next depends a great deal on the way you choose to live your current life. Listen to your heart and do what's right. Don't believe you can cheat your fate; karma cannot be fooled. Be honest and loving and you will find, 'It's getting better all the time.'"[10]

"She's completely crazy," Mr. W told Martha after the meeting had broken up.

"Isn't that what they said about Cassandra?" she asked.

"No, they just didn't believe a word she said," he replied.

"What good is knowing something," Martha wondered, "if you're not going to be believed?"

---

[10] "Sgt. Pepper's Lonely Hearts Club Band," The Beatles

CHAPTER 26

THE THINGS WE DO FOR LOVE

The vote on the merger of the two churches was a mere formality. In fact, only five votes were cast out of a possible twelve—four, firmly in favor of the merger. (I cast the only nay vote on account of being a firm contrarian and believing that any group that would have me wasn't worth joining.)[11]

The future of the Dianic Wiccan Church of Lilith lay in the outcome of the vote for high priestess. Those ladies who wanted the church to represent peaceful noncompliance with the patriarchy would vote for me. Those who wanted the violent overthrow of the patriarchy would vote for Cathy Anderson.

"Don't let her draw you into a political discussion," Martha advised. "If you outthink her, the crowd will think you are a bully."

---

[11] I don't know whether to give credit to Mark Twain or Groucho Marx. Take your pick.

"And, for God's sake, don't make her cry," Starr said. "She's already ten times better-looking than you. Don't give her the sympathy votes, too."

"Thanks, Starr. You know, I've seen her naked a lot more often than you have."

"Don't be too sure."

"Don't bring up your past together," the little brunette told me. She was holding a clipboard and checking items off a list as we spoke. "The general consensus among lesbians and straights both is that, when Cathy was a confused eighteen-year-old innocent, you seduced her and led her into a summer of BDSM."

"She was the queen; I was the slave girl. I mean, *duh*!"

There was to be one face-off before the voting commenced. It was not as much a debate as it was a fashion show. I had chosen for my high priestess gown a sleek, shiny little number. It was short and cut off on one shoulder. I was told it was a Grisogono. (I had Connie try it on first. She's not my size, but I wasn't taking any chances.)

Cathy's dress was pink and frilly and built like a tent from the waist down. She could have had a den of cub scouts camping out down there. (I'm glad she hid her gams. Her long, shapely legs are a definite ten, while my brown, muscular legs are an eight, at best.)

Cathy spoke first. She donned a pair of reading glasses to make herself look more intellectual. I was sure the lenses were clear. Her eyesight, like everything else about her, is perfect.

She read her cue cards robotically. "The Church of Lilith forbids male membership now and forever."

Since the beginning of the human race, there have not been two girls who hate men more than Lilith and me. Nevertheless, I agree with Lilith that the church should be open to well-meaning men who respect women.

"Women who are married to men must divorce them immediately."

Well, there was no way this was going to fly. Some males are frisky and fun. I've had a couple of male dogs, and I know I couldn't just leave them behind.

"Health care and education will be provided free for the children of all members. If a woman wants to raise her own children, she may do so."

That meant, if a mom wanted her own kids, she was going to have to work full-time to care for them.

"IVF and other alternative fertilization methods will be paid for by the church."

Cathy went on for almost an hour describing a female Utopia where women could have careers and children both. There was to be an army of caretakers (the Dianic Army) as well as an army for defense against masculine aggression (the Amazon Army).

Our seats all faced the back of the church where the stage was. There was a loud crash of broken glass behind us. A woman rushed up to Cathy and whispered in her ear. Cathy went off script for the first time. "The ladies who are arranging my coronation have informed me that we are in some danger, and we are going to have to cut things short. For reasons I'm not too clear on, we were initially going to pretend there was to be an election. That farce, I'm happy to say, can now be dropped from the program."

"Now, just a minute, Your Highness. Hold on there." I could see that Cathy was in full "Catherine of Aragon" mode. I approached the dais in a friendly but determined manner. "I'm not willing to concede just yet," I said.

There were screams behind us as the front doors were smashed open and dozens of wild-eyed Fred Swink supporters poured into the church brandishing pitchforks and tire irons.

"Kill them witches!" one yelled.

"Yeah, but first strip 'em necked to see if they have the sign of the devil on 'em," another cried.

"See if they got a third nipple!" a little tweeny in pigtails (who shouldn't have been there) said.

At some unseen signal, the choir stood and removed their robes, revealing the AK-47s hidden beneath.

People who saw me force Cathy down behind the pulpit later spoke of my heroism. The fact is, I wanted to get credit for stopping this maelstrom before it became murderous.

"Just a goll dern minute!" I yelled into the microphone.

There was a loud thud to the right of me and I turned to see Evie landing from a jump from the balcony. It wasn't the sexy, fun-loving little Evie I knew, though. This Evie had gone over to the side of madness. Her eyes were crazed, and she barely seemed to notice that she had broken her foot. "*Death to tyrants!*" she cried and aimed a derringer at me.

Before I could register what had happened, Nan Butler had jumped in front of me. The bullet from the derringer went right through Nan and hit my sternum.

Nan had evidently fired her service pistol, and Evie flew back into the congregation with a bullet hole right between her eyes. Blood was pumping out of Nan's chest like a red geyser.

"*No!*" I screamed. I cradled her in my arms. I put pressure on the wound. I tried to force the blood back inside her.

"Help!" I begged.

Then, I guess I went a little crazy. I tried to cup the blood coming out of my chest and pour it into Nan's wound.

There was an undefinable moment in time when it was just Nan and me. It probably lasted no more than a second, but it was timeless to us. I told her how I wished I'd met her when I was innocent and pure like her, and she told me her love for me was the most beautiful thing she had ever experienced in her lifetime. We had a perfect rapport, a perfect understanding of each other. For that second, day, year, lifetime … we were one.

Then shots were fired, and Starr threw me roughly to the floor of the stage. I passed out for a while, and when I woke up, it was all over. I was strapped in a gurney, and EMTs were rolling me out.

"Nan?" I asked weakly.

A pretty young girl named Dawn Hightower was standing next to me. She was wearing a bloody T-shirt with a peace sign on it.

"She passed peacefully in my arms," she told me. "Her last words were, 'You have very soft titties.'"

Printed in the United States
by Baker & Taylor Publisher Services